A Country of Refuge

EDITED BY
Lucy Popescu

unbound

This edition first published in 2016

Unbound
6th Floor Mutual House, 70 Conduit Street, London W1S 2GF
www.unbound.co.uk

Text Design by PDQ

A CIP record for this book is available from the British Library

ISBN 978-1-78352-268-2 (trade paperback)
ISBN 978-1-78352-269-9 (ebook)
ISBN 978-1-78352-293-4 (limited edition)

Printed in Great Britain by Clays Ltd, St Ives Plc.

1 2 3 4 5 6 7 8 9

To my late mother Christine and her sisters Diana and Josephine Pullein-Thompson who taught me the importance of compassion and the power of words.

With special thanks

Faz Fazeli
Elisa Segrave

Dear Reader,

The book you are holding came about in a rather different way to most others. It was funded directly by readers through a new website: Unbound. Unbound is the creation of three writers. We started the company because we believed there had to be a better deal for both writers and readers. On the Unbound website, authors share the ideas for the books they want to write directly with readers. If enough of you support the book by pledging for it in advance, we produce a beautifully bound special subscribers' edition and distribute a regular edition and e-book wherever books are sold, in shops and online.

This new way of publishing is actually a very old idea (Samuel Johnson funded his dictionary this way). We're just using the internet to build each writer a network of patrons. Here, at the back of this book, you'll find the names of all the people who made it happen.

Publishing in this way means readers are no longer just passive consumers of the books they buy, and authors are free to write the books they really want. They get a much fairer return too – half the profits their books generate, rather than a tiny percentage of the cover price.

If you're not yet a subscriber, we hope that you'll want to join our publishing revolution and have your name listed in one of our books in the future. To get you started, here is a £5 discount on your first pledge. Just visit unbound.com, make your pledge and type **country** in the promo code box when you check out.

Thank you for your support,

Dan, Justin and John
Founders, Unbound

Contents

A Country of Refuge

Lucy Popescu

INTRODUCTION

Britain has a long history as a country of refuge for those fleeing conflict, poverty or terror, and this is something we should be proud of. The 1951 Refugee Convention guarantees everybody the right to apply for asylum. It has saved millions of lives. No country has ever withdrawn from it. And yet most of the refugee stories we read about in the media are negative. There is a growing anti-immigrant rhetoric and many politicians fuel these prejudices here in the UK and elsewhere. Refugees are falsely labelled 'economic migrants' or, worse, are accused of harbouring terrorists.

I work closely with refugees as a volunteer mentor with Write to Life, Freedom from Torture's creative writing programme. The charity (formerly the Medical Foundation for the Care of Victims of Torture) was founded by Helen Bamber in 1985, to provide refugees and asylum seekers with medical treatment, counselling and therapy and to document evidence of torture. I joined Write to Life in 2010 and was immediately struck by the resilience and humour of the group. The stories I hear are about the emotional scars of torture, the pain of leaving behind loved ones and the struggles of building a new life. Imagine the sheer loneliness of sitting in a room for days or weeks on end without anyone to talk to, with nothing you hold dear, nothing that is familiar. No friends, no family. You know you are lucky to be alive, but the solitude is crushing. This is the reality for many of the refugees I know. Some have forged new lives for themselves but the relentless struggle to assimilate, to integrate in a new, often alien, culture takes its toll. Some have been forced to leave their children behind, some are coping with bereavement, some have lost their entire family. Few are able to practise their original occupations – teachers, academics, writers, lawyers, journalists, accountants… Most refugees and asylum seekers are desperate to return home, as soon as the situation in their country has improved.

I first conceived of this project in January 2014, months before the current European refugee crisis. I had just received a copy of *A Country Too Far* (published by Penguin Australia), a superb collection of fiction, memoir, poetry and essays, co-edited by Rosie Scott and Tom Keneally, which aimed to set the record straight about asylum seekers in Australia and protest their government's treatment of them. Inspired, I sent out a flurry of emails, swiftly got some terrific writers on board and immediately set about trying to find a suitable publisher. My wonderful agent, Andrew Lownie, approached a number of mainstream publishers but drew a blank. I then spent a further year trying the smaller, independent presses with no success. Fortunately, in June 2015 the pioneering Unbound Books came on board and I agreed to crowdfund and pay the contributors' fees myself.

A Country of Refuge is comprised of short fiction, poems, memoirs and essays. I wanted the writers to focus on the experiences of refugees and asylum seekers in an attempt to directly challenge the negative press and to cast a more positive light on a situation that, for many, is a living hell. The contributions have exceeded all my expectations: original, enlightening, knowledgeable and profound.

Sadly, there will always be people in need of a safe haven – it is a common plight and a timeless theme which

I think Sebastian Barry perfectly captures in his short story that opens the anthology. 'Fragment of a Journal, Author Unknown' recalls Ireland's famine years in the nineteenth century, when tens of thousands of starving people risked voyages across the Atlantic in hazardous 'coffin ships'. Many disturbing parallels can be drawn between the exodus of the famine years and the current refugee crisis.

I include two heart-rending stories by Roma Tearne, one about Sri Lanka, the other about Iraq, which chillingly illustrate the circumstances that force people to flee their homeland. Marina Lewycka's 'A Hard-Luck Story', narrated from the point of view of a cynical guard at a detention centre, explores the horrific reality for many refugees whose stories are not believed and who are then sent home. In 'Selfie' Stephen Kelman's ambivalent narrator comes face to face with a migrant selling selfie sticks in Rome and wonders 'if anybody loved this man and told him so before he left. It would seem such a long way to come without love.' Courttia Newland's evocative story, 'The Road to Silvertown', imagines a time when British citizens might one day find it necessary to flee to a country like Syria by foot and boat. Amanda Craig's brilliant satire, 'Metamorphosis 2', describes a similar journey but from a very different perspective. There is also poignant fiction from Moris Farhi and Sue Gee, provocative tales by Tim Finch, A. L. Kennedy and Rose Tremain, and illuminating poems from Elaine Feinstein, Hubert Moore and Ruth Padel.

Some of the contributors come from refugee or immigrant backgrounds themselves. In his bitter-sweet memoir, 'The Dog-Shaped Hole in the Garden', Hassan Abdulrazzak looks back at his family's departure from Iraq and their arrival in the UK. Because members of his family were associated with the Iraqi Communist Party, the main opposition to Saddam Hussein's Ba'ath party, they were forced into exile. They eventually found a safe haven here.

Writing about her family history, Katharine Quarmby draws parallels with today's refugees and ponders what 'becoming English' really means. Nick Barlay, in his account of his parents' flight from Hungary in 1956, observes that 'those who flee bullets have only one thing on their minds: how to cross the first border they come to'.

I also invited reflections on the history of immigration. Alex Wheatle's story, 'Alfred and Vincent', based on his father's experiences, reminds us of a time when Britain actively sought migrant labour. Wheatle describes a period in the 1950s when Jamaican immigrants were welcomed to these shores to help rebuild after the Second World War. Hanif Kureishi's 'These Mysterious Strangers: The New Story of the Immigrant' could just as well be about the paranoia surrounding refugees today as it is about perceptions of the immigrant as a 'threatening other... a source of contagion and horror'.

The essays in this collection also provide a valuable political context and suggest what needs to change. Kate Clanchy's incisive piece illuminates some of the horrors witnessed by children who grow up in a war zone and illustrates how, once safe, writing can help them process this trauma. More needs to be done to help vulnerable refugees and this is why Freedom from Torture's therapeutic work is so important. History often repeats itself and Joan Smith draws interesting parallels between the plights of Anne Frank's family and that of Aylan Kurdi. Both their fathers, Otto Frank and Abdullah Shenu (Kurdi), tried desperately and failed to find refuge in a safe country: 'Aylan Kurdi did not need to die, any more than Anne Frank', she argues. 'Seventy years apart, their stories are characterised by the same depressingly bureaucratic response to refugees fleeing fascist regimes. The closing of borders to refugees from Nazi Germany is mirrored in the twenty-first century by legal obstacles which force desperate people into the hands of criminal gangs.'

People fleeing persecution may have to use irregular means in order to escape and claim asylum in another country. The media is quick to expose what it or the Home Office perceives as 'illegal' or 'bogus' asylum seekers. In her eloquent essay, 'A Time to Lie', Noo Saro-Wiwa explores how traumatised refugees are sometimes forced to tell a half-truth or 'innocent lies' because they fear the truth will not be believed. She points out: 'The asylum seeker born out of shoddy bureaucracy often struggles to prove not only their identity but their ill-treatment too. The policemen who dragged them into African prison cells don't always fill out paperwork. Those same police might not maintain records of a gang rape reported to them by a distraught girl.' As Saro-Wiwa warns: 'Today's paradises could become the purgatories of tomorrow. Which is why it's best to treat others the way we would like them to treat us.'

William Boyd's letters about Noo's father, Ken Saro-Wiwa, executed in 1995 on the orders of Nigeria's General Sani Abacha, underline the fact that it is often writers, journalists, opposition leaders – dissident voices – who are in the front line and the first to be silenced or forced into exile. The role of artists and writers in effecting change is a theme taken up by A. L. Kennedy in her rousing essay that concludes the anthology. Kennedy observes: 'True art is not an indulgence, but a fundamental defence of humanity.' She goes on to argue that writers, in particular, have a duty to respond to the media, propaganda and public opinion as 'guardians of imagination, of wider thought, of culture' because, she warns, 'Imagination is, on all sides, apparently failing. And when it fails, it fails us all.'

Like Kennedy, I believe writers are uniquely placed to challenge pre-conceived ideas and stereotypes because of their understanding of the power of words and their ability to articulate truths. I want *A Country of Refuge* to demonstrate that 'art is stronger than propaganda', compassion a more vital force than distrust. It has been a long journey to get this anthology in the public domain and I hope it will make a positive contribution to the current debate and foster a kinder attitude towards our fellow humans who are fleeing violence, persecution, poverty or intolerance. I've found all the contributions immensely readable and hope you do too.

Lucy Popescu
January 2016

Sebastian Barry

FRAGMENT OF A JOURNAL, AUTHOR UNKNOWN

The sad truth of hard times is there are few heroes. It was our own people knocked our cabin. The Peelers that came with them up the valley were Dublin boys. The landlord never made an appearance at all for he did not need to. He could get anyone he liked to do anything he liked because he had the pennies and they did not. Looking back it seems to me that you will never save a starving people with committees and yet that is what was attempted. The committee to do this and the committee to do that and then the people dying in the margins between. The poorhouse in Westport so full to the brim that only death made room for more entrants. The feverhouse behind the great building a factory of suffering and hopelessness. It is hard to look back and tell what was to be seen.

My father came in from the valley when his place was knocked and went into Louisburgh because he was told the Poor Law Guardians would be there and he could ask for a ticket. The little town of Louisburgh was also full to bursting like it was a fair day but it wasn't for a fair day. Then the desolate crowd was told that the Guardians had gone on up to Delphi Lodge in their side-car and my father would be obliged to follow after. We were just two wretches holding a hand each, myself and my brother, and of course our mother was dead. She died on the cabin floor like a mouse melting after being hit with a shoe. She went black as a weed in November. Up we went my father and ourselves with about three hundred others to see the Guardians. You might not know that district and it is all mountains and cold valleys and rivers as black as dried blood. Way up the head of the mountains is a fine house called Delphi Lodge. That's where the gentlemen were having their lunch. We waited out on the lawns in front of the house while they ate. I won't even say when was the last time any of us saw food. The truth is my father was ashamed of our emergency and all the long traipse he never spoke a word. He was a proud man in his way that had worked his quarter acre like a Trojan for long hard years. Now he was nothing and blowing with his own sons along the road like the curling leaves of autumn. At length the Guardians came forth and bid us return to Louisburgh and clear off the lawns because the tickets for the poorhouse were below. We had come many miles to hear that. So with a great and strange sighing the whole body of emaciated people turned from the cold windows and back we went the way we had come. Snow and its sister icy rain lashed against us and many started to fall, weak as they were. Mothers went down and children and then even my father stumbled and down he went. He went down like a shot dog and never to rise. I went on with my brother Jamie following the buffeted crowd and by some strange grace we got back to Louisburgh.

The next day we got our tickets for Westport. It was a seven hour walk across the mountains and by exactly the same narrow track we had come. The sun because it has no sense of occasion had risen clear and bright as it sometimes does in an Irish autumn and all along the way we saw little humps of people, women with their long ruined faces, and babies and children frozen and starved into death. A glaze of frost threw its fancy lace across their limbs. We passed them as if we were beings of another world called the living. Out past Delphi Lodge the country became so desolate God Himself had never visited. It had neither character nor location but seemed merely a blank district of nowhere. Jamie and myself went on and even our hardened feet began to swell and crack. We came down into Westport and proceeded to the poorhouse but though we had tickets they were useless. In front of the poorhouse was a crowd so immense they made a music like a lamentation of the mad.

By some instinct I cannot identify I brought Jamie to the quay and when night fell we crept onto one of the old ships that we hoped would carry us away. There were men selling passage on the ship. We had no money so I judged it would be beneficent to stow away. Now you will realise that we had stowed away on Hell's cargo vessel. The passengers numbered about three hundred on a boat designed for at most a hundred. It had maybe forty berths. The people were obliged to bring on whatever provisions they could muster because the master had no food stowed for them. Water was to be two cups a day and it seemed like water taken from a black drain. The hatches were locked and never to be opened and so began four weeks of filth, destitution, misery and death. There are no gods and no priests for such a people. We were nothing and so nothing needed to be done for us. The hold remained closed and pitch-black and storms were only to be endured. Empty bellies vomited the last froth of life and we shat and pissed where we lay. The bilges rolled with every type of human liquid. The air was air that could only have pleased Beelzebub. All around me people died in a simple conclusion of calamity. Efforts were made in the dark to eat whatever was to be eaten. The abysm of suffering reached has not been described in human history because it would disgust and repel any reader. No camera could capture it because all took place in utter darkness as if we were already deceased and we were being punished for terrible sins. Our sin was that we were poor and therefore nothing. Our sin was that we were too many in the eyes of government and that it would be a blessing on the country if we were to perish. In this way we were described as a plague on our country and nothing more than vermin and rats. Now a sensible and resourceful God was visiting destruction on us to rid the world of a colossal nuisance. Will I tell you that Jamie died beside me, a boy of some seven years? I felt for his body in the darkness and touched his cold form. His body was lying in a shallow lake of filth. That was his burial place, the dark hold of history.

Then up we came into the waters by Quebec and the long nails were pulled from the boards of the hatches and light came into the hold like a pour of water. Bleak eyes reflected it like fireflies in some adamantine region. What had been women stared out as if their minds were cancelled. Men raised their skeletal forms and tried to stand. Everywhere around me were corpses and corpses with the ship's rats using them unimpeded. These small black ministers scampered away into the deeper bilges at the flooding of the light. A ladder was let down and the survivors were brought up onto the deck. Sailors themselves had died of fevers caught from us and even the master himself was dead. The ship's owner had got his money and the brokers had made their profits and they cared neither for cargo nor crew. Profit in such circumstances is surely on the highest spot on the tabulation of evil. On the list of deeds that cannot be forgiven in any court of man or God.

Quebec was in that time in a great terror about these famished nothings because all we had to offer this new place was a great clamour for assistance. But we were calling out, it seemed to them, from a region of virulent fever and indeed contagion had already burned through the town and further out into the countryside as if demons were firing heather. Their solution was to herd us into long wooden sheds. Pastors and women almost insane in their bravery came in to us where we lay on the hundreds of pallets. Efforts were made to feed us and yet many were now beyond the benefit of food. The bodies were carted off and let down into pits. No place on earth it seemed could have wanted us and all behind were coming another thousand ships heaving with their melancholy freight. Humanity had slipped away from us and it was as if the candles of our souls had been snuffed out. We had made our desperate attempt to escape the pestilence of hunger but because we were nothing nothing could be done for us.

Ireland/Quebec/1847

Elaine Feinstein
MIGRATIONS

1

In late March, birds from the Gambia,
white throat warblers, who wintered in
the branches of a feathery acacia;
Mandelstam's goldfinch; pink foot
geese from the Arctic. All
arrive using the stars, along
flyways old as Homer and Jeremiah.

2

Avian immigration is down this year,
but humans still have reasons to move on,
the usual chronicle of poverty, enemies,
or ominous skies the colour of tobacco.
They arrive in London with battered luggage,
and eyes dark as black cherries

holding fast to old religions
and histories, remembering
the shock of being hunted in the streets,
the pain at leaving their dead
in broken cemeteries, their resilience
hardwired as birds' skill in navigation.

On the Jubilee line, a black woman
has the profile of a wood carving from Benin.
In Willesden Green, *Polski delikatesy*, or a grocer
piling up African vegetables. An English woman
buys hot ginger and white radish: the filigree
of migration, symbiosis, assimilation.

3

All my grandparents came from Odessa
a century ago, spoke little English,
and were doubtless suspect as foreigners
—probably anarchist or Bolshevik—
very likely to be dreaming of bombs.
It is never easy to be a stranger,

to be split between loneliness
and disloyalty, to be impatient
with dogma, yet still distrusted
in a world which prefers to be secular.
When I listen to the gaiety of Klezmer,
I understand why migrants like ghettos.

These people come from desperate countries
where flies walk over the faces of sick children,
and even here in Britain the luckless
will find gangmasters to arrange
work in mudflats as cockle pickers.
Why should they care my ancestors

had a long history of crossing borders,
when I am settled now after all those journeys?
And why do I want to make common cause
with them anyway? Only because I remember
how easily the civil world turns brutal.
If it does, we shall have the same enemies.

Roma Tearne
THE BLUE SCARF

Kirthika is in the shop. I can see her from where I'm sitting, picking up a scarf and looking at herself in the mirror. By the way she holds the thing up I know she isn't interested in it. She puts the scarf down and picks up another. This one is a dirty sludgy brown, like the melting snow outside. I stare. Kirthika likes bright colours. She is a lone magpie in that respect. The brown scarf is a clear indication of her mood. The shop assistant must have sensed her lack of seriousness too because I see her walk towards Kirthika. I see Kirthika shake her head and imagine she would be smiling slightly. I look down at the newspaper I'm pretending to read and the words blur. I need an eye test, I think. When I look up again Kirthika has gone. I see her figure hurrying off in the direction of the coffee shop.

We are in the airport. We arrived at six. It isn't an easy journey from where we live. First you take a bus to the town of Yur. Then you walk to the train station. Then you take the express train to the airport. This bit is the most comfortable part of the trip. It is warm, swift and allows you a little time to dream. The train today was empty. Kirthika and I sat staring out of the window at the frozen, flat landscape backlit by a dull bluish light. This is all the light we are permitted at this time of year although the snow sometimes gives a boost to it. There wasn't much snow this morning, just a little rain melting and distorting the view from the train. Once or twice Kirthika had run her hand across the window in order to see the name of the station we were passing. Otherwise she didn't move. We did not talk. The plane we were due to meet was currently flying somewhere over the Middle East.

Kirthika is wearing a sari I don't remember having seen before. I first noticed it on the train and wondered if it was new. Where did she get the money from to buy it? I frowned. My wife is a very careful woman where money is concerned. I can't imagine her going out and buying clothes at this juncture. Perhaps my memory was failing and I had seen it but just can't remember. In any case, I thought, staring out at the hard white landscape, where would she get a sari from, in this part of the world?

'Why are you smiling?' she asked.

I shook my head not knowing how to explain the irony of my thoughts.

'Lillian will bring saris for you,' I had said instead.

Lillian is our daughter-in-law. At this moment, if my calculations are right she will be staring down at a place unmarked on any map, sitting next to our son, holding onto the baby who would, hopefully, be asleep. The baby, our only grandson, is one year old. We have not met him yet. Sitting on the train I saw that Kirthika had the same thought. I saw it flit across her mind like a flash of blue light. Like lightning, gone as swiftly as it surfaced. Suppressed. Earthed. Kirthika has an expressive face. She can't fool me. But all she said was,

'I hope not. They have much more important things to bring in their luggage.'

Than a sari for the mother-in-law that Lillian has never met, she means.

It is four years since we last saw our son. A lot has happened in that time. For a start he met his future wife one month after we left. Perhaps it was grief that left him open to the possibilities of love. Our departure was brutal enough to make this happen. Until then no girl had really interested him. It was all work, until then.

Our train had passed the town of Aavig as I was thinking this, with its small empty railway station. I caught a glimpse of a man walking a dog, a postman riding his bicycle, a truck. Behind the shorn trees there was a glint of a frozen river. And then we left the town and the church spires and the houses all huddled together. In summer this is a place of scenic beauty. Now it goes in a moment, swallowed up by the speed of the train.

When we left our home on the island it had been dawn with a light not dissimilar to this one. Only it was hot, and there was a tropical breeze lifting thankfully off the sea. The moon, like a fingernail paring, had been still in the sky watching us move softly, backwards and forwards from the house to the car. We had kept only one light on at the time for fear of alerting the neighbours. Or anyone in the pay of the army thugs. My throat had been dry, my mind alternating with thoughts of what I should not forget and other, irrelevant things. Even today, four years later I can reproduce that dry, uncrying feeling.

'Where are the passports?' Kirthika had murmured. 'Have you got them?'

'Yes, in my bag. In the folder,' I murmured back.

Our son walked outside with one of the suitcases. His soft crunch on the gravel made me wince. Walking was dangerous. Talking was dangerous. A cigarette glowing could be the death of you. Four forty-five, I remember thinking. And that was when I had looked up at the sky and seen the fingernail of a moon. The catamarans would be coming in from the sea, the sarongs of the fishermen slapping against their legs, wet from the water; the air smelling sweetly of wind, the sand soft and unmarked, and empty. There were three boats that came in regularly to this little inlet. I knew all of them. I knew the names of the fishermen, I knew their wives. Kirthika, the local doctor, had been present when the babies were born. Two of them had been named after her. And now we were leaving.

'Give me the other bag,' Kirthika said. 'I want to check something.'

'Mama, you can't take the goraka,' our son told her. 'They won't let you and you don't want to create a fuss at the airport.'

'No,' Kirthika agreed.

And she put the jar on the dining table. I stared at it. Normally she would not have given in so easily. Normally she would not have put anything on the table either, without so much as a mat under it. The dining table was made of soft satinwood and was her pride and joy. We had bought it many years before on an impulse. Everyone had advised us not to.

'Satinwood marks easily,' they said.

'It's too expensive,' they said.

'It is a sacred tree. Used for coffins. It brings its own bad luck with it,' they had said.

'The servants will ruin it,' they said.

'Don't do it!' Kirthika's mother said.

But we did. Before I could stop myself I wondered, was this the reason we were having to leave, now. Nonsense walked the night, grinning at me, ghoulishly. I am a rational man, but still, I am capable of ridiculous moments.

Instead of packing my last bag I went into the kitchen and filled a clay jug with cold water. Then I watered the plants in my study. I was aware that my son was watching me, helplessly.

'Papa,' he said at last. 'Don't worry about the plants.'

But I was worried about them. They were my plants, still. They belonged here. And because of this, they were sacred. Like the fishermen, like the white bleached sand on the beach, soft as the hair of a newborn. Like the horizon line between sea and sky and the jasmine flowers that bloomed no matter what violent thing was going on across the veranda. It all belonged to this land. I put my hand out and touched the small statue of Lord Buddha that Kirthika had placed beside that of Lord Krishna. I could hear my heart beating. I thought it might be breaking.

'Have we time for a walk?' Kirthika asked.

She had come up silently behind me and had seen me touch the statue. She refrained from comment. In the past she told me not to be an unbeliever. In the past I told her that Buddhism was not a religion but a philosophy. And anyway religion was a toy played with by people who were full of fear. These days neither of us have such conversations. That sort of discussion was an indulgence. Now both of us compress and fold our speech. Leaving many things unsaid. Now less is irrevocably more.

'No,' I said, finally.

'Please,' Kirthika asked. 'I want one last walk.'

In all the years of our marriage I have never refused her anything.

'All right,' I said.

'Are you crazy?' our son asked, his eyes wide.

I had heard my heart beating again, and again had wondered if it would break. But the human heart is stronger than that, I think now, remembering.

'Someone will see you,' our son said. 'Then all this will have been for nothing.'

His face was on the edge of grief.

'All right then,' his mother agreed but I had made up my mind.

It was our last chance. Our only moment. We would have to live off it forever.

'Let's go,' I said, adding, for our son's benefit, 'we'll go out through the back. No one will see us.'

I didn't wait for his reply but took Kirthika's hand and we left through the back door.

It was cool on the beach. And empty. The fishermen had already gone leaving only the marks from their boats in a long unbroken line on the sand. We stood, half hidden by a coconut tree, and stared out to sea. Stared at the thin blue line that signified eternity. I sensed without hearing that Kirthika was crying but I didn't turn round. I knew what she was thinking.

That on this beach a girl was raped by the army. That on this beach a man was killed. That blood was spilt in our name and the names of all the people of this island. That we loved this place. That nowhere else on earth would ever be home. Eyes, I thought, look your last.

Further up the coast a festival was in progress. The rich and the famous from Western nations were in attendance. For a few brief days they too could stand looking at the horizon line. But they would never see what we saw in that moment. They could not love this land as passionately as we did. How could the tailorbird's call signify anything special to them? For us it is the birdsong of childhood, heralding a lullaby at twilight, a mother's hand stroking her son's head. Part of a young girl's dreams. No, the tailorbird could not mean all this to the visitors on the island.

Kirthika was crying in earnest by now. From the corner of my eye I saw her, head bent, like a young girl. Like the girl from long ago, whose hand I had so insistently asked for in marriage. We did not know then the things we know now.

'We'd better go,' I told her.

The sea moved restlessly and somewhere in the distance a train rushed past.

'Come, Kiri,' I said. 'Come, come.'

And we went back to the house, our footprints in the sand. We were people who had seen too much and must therefore be killed.

Our son had wanted to drive us to the airport but I refused in case we were followed. He would have had to make the return journey, alone. In my home it is a well-known fact that people are killed in road 'accidents'. Best to say our goodbyes in the house. And when it came to it we were strangely calm.

'Please lie low,' Kirthika told our son.

She spoke as if she was telling him his food was in the fridge. As if she would be back after her shift at the hospital. As if this was an ordinary day. Understanding this he joined in the charade.

'Yes,' he agreed. 'Ring when you get there.'

'Don't worry if it takes a little while. There might be a problem with the phone.'

He nodded.

'And you mustn't worry either,' he told her, 'I might be out of range. Don't assume that anything...'

'Yes,' his mother and I said in unison.

There followed a pause as first his mother, and then I, embraced him. In all those years of loving him never once had we dreamed it would come to this; that we should leave our only child, defenceless and alone, in his own home.

'We'll get you out as soon as we can,' I said. 'You know that, don't you?'

'Of course, Papa. Of course. You don't have to say it. I understand.'

We nodded. And then we went. Closing the beloved door for the very last time.

In the car going to the airport I didn't tell Kirthika what I had done. She had too many other things to deal with. It was only later that I told her about the photographs in my suitcase. The ones I had taken when they raped the girl, when they decapitated the men, when they shot the aid worker. The secret photographs that I would smuggle out to the West and send around the world. But going to the airport I said nothing. Sitting in the front with the driver I listened only to the air rushing past. The fingernail moon followed us like a blessing. How bright it seemed. We passed a sign directing traffic to the festival that was taking place in Galle. I had been told that big banks were supporting the event; that money went where money exists. That life at the top was marvellous. We too lived life at the top once until I stooped to listen to other people's stories, until the pity of what was happening was too much for us. When the phone call came issuing the first death threat we were unprepared.

'Maybe I should stop,' I told Kirthika, belatedly. 'They are stronger than we are.'

'What use is the human heart if it cannot feel for others?' Kirthika replied.

She despised violence. She was a woman who saved lives daily.

'The most noble grace the gods can bestow on a man is the gift of empathy,' she said.

In her presence I quaked. She is a wonderful woman, my wife.

'Speak, memory!'

So I spoke. And now we are leaving. Oh hold still my heart.

That day, at the airport we went, numbed, through security. Foreign visitors moved about, talking quietly in English. The overhead address called out an endless list of flights. Dubai, Karachi, Singapore, Bangkok, Adelaide, Melbourne, Calgary. We listened mesmerised feeling small, defenceless. London, Rome, Paris, Frankfurt, the tannoy continued before coming to the name we dreaded hearing. Stockholm. The smiles of the Sri Lankan girls were for the foreigners, the rich, the famous; those born under a lucky star. Is this how the Jews had felt? When all in Germany turned their faces against them?

We were asked to take our shoes off, to hold our arms

out, to be checked for sharp objects. The man who stared at our passports had an expressionless face. I still remember. Briefly I wondered what his life was like. Two women passengers went past swiftly. They were talking of all the wonderful things they hadn't had time to see.

'Never mind,' one said. 'We can always come again.'

We held out our boarding passes. I remembered how I had been someone important once, a man with a house, in the most beautiful place in the world. Once, people turned to me for help. Now as I stored our luggage in the overhead locker I told myself, I was nobody. And then, in hardly a moment, with thrust and push of engines, as our plane rose to meet the moon, I held Kirthika's hand tightly in mine. And it was she, my wife, who comforted me.

That had been four years ago. Four years of living in this foreign land. Four years of darkness, of intermittent word from our son, of constant worry over him. We grew old, Kirthika and I, belonging nowhere, talking to other refugees, haltingly, sketching our story, listening to theirs, knowing that language was not enough to express all we felt. Sometimes, in the dead of night, alone in bed, we would speak together in Tamil. It is only possible to speak of what is most precious in your mother tongue. A refugee from the Congo told us, a child hears the first words of love at a woman's breast. So in those lonely moments together it was in Tamil that we spoke of our son. Of his forthcoming marriage.

'She's a fine girl, Papa. I love her.'

'And does she love you too, son?' his mother had asked.

'Oh yes! And she sends her love to you, too!'

And then, later, after the wedding we could not attend, nine months later, another late night phone call.

'It's a boy!'

'Healthy?'

'Yes, yes.'

'And his mother?'

'All doing fine!'

'Congratulations!'

He did not want to spoil the moment by telling us that the threats had begun again. That one of his colleagues had been mysteriously cut down on his way to work, that a Russian girl had been raped in the South and an innocent man working for the Red Cross had been shot defending her. What he told us instead was how the tailorbird had sung its lullaby to the newborn child.

'Remember, Mama,' he said. 'You told me how that bird sang when I was born!'

Sitting on the train this morning, staring at the bleak landscape, these are the thoughts I had. Our son is flying out of a dawn, leaving paradise, joining the great migration of our century.

'Will they be over Poland by now?' Kirthika had asked.

'No, no. Not yet. The Middle East, perhaps.'

She nodded and went back to staring out of the window.

'I meant to ask him to pack some milk rice,' she murmured but then she gave me a quick apologetic look.

Old habits die hard, her look said. Kirthika misses many things. Her unspoken longings are so great that I can hardly bear them. She knows, as I do, that our son, though safe at last, will not be happy. That his wife will be thinking of those she has had to leave behind. A mother, a father, a younger brother who is constantly harassed by the army. A younger sister who lives in fear. An older sister who *was* raped. So no; our son will not be happy. Our gain is his wife's loss.

At the airport we had gone to the arrivals lounge immediately and I bought a newspaper. When I handed over the change I saw my hand was shaking. Kirthika saw this too and decided to go off on her own for a bit. I sat down. That's when I saw her trying on the scarf. It is six forty-five in the morning, now. The eighteenth of January. Four years, three months and seventeen days since we last saw our son. The palms of my hands are sweating. Kirthika is a long time at the coffee shop. The seconds hand on my watch moves jerkily. Six forty-six. Their plane is due at any moment. Where is Kirthika, I think, irritated. I glance up at the arrivals board. Nothing there, of course.

'I'm here,' she says, suddenly from behind me.

To my amazement I see she has bought a scarf after all. It is bright blue, like the sea we left behind. Blue, for the little boy who is arriving.

'I shall wear it for him,' Kirthika says, casually. 'Not every day we have a grandchild visiting.'

I nod. I want to hug her, this brave, beautiful wife of mine.

'It was reduced,' she admits. 'That's why I bought it.'

Like our circumstances. I get my mobile phone out.

'It's charged up?'

'Yes, yes.'

We wait. People come and are met. There are cries of welcome in Swedish. Lone men in grey suits walk hurriedly out to waiting taxis, a black man sweeps the floor, another stands holding up a sign. A family comes out, a mother, a father, two children. One of the children is crying and the father bends down and speaks to her. He catches my eye and smiles faintly then shrugs.

'Long flight!' he says, in Swedish.

I smile back just as the telephone rings.

'Answer it, answer it,' Kirthika says.

I press all the wrong buttons but then we connect and I hear my son's voice.

'Papa,' he says, his voice tired. 'We are here. Our connecting flight is in half an hour.'

'Are you okay?'

'We're all fine. You know we can't come out, don't you?'

'We know, don't worry. We just wanted to... you know... be in the same building... oh here's your mother...'

Kirthika is talking. I hear her tell our daughter-in-law she is wearing a new scarf in honour of the little boy. I hear her laugh, a high, tense laugh. I hear her ask our daughter-in-law if she is all right, and I hear her blow a kiss into the phone. Then she switches it off.

'They have to hurry,' she tells me, her eyes shining. 'Or they'll miss their connecting flight. But they'll ring when they get to London.'

I nod once more. And in the train going back Kirthika tells me,

'Annay, I heard the little one's voice, faintly. Just like a small bird!'

Hanif Kureishi

THESE MYSTERIOUS STRANGERS: THE NEW STORY OF THE IMMIGRANT

The immigrant has become a contemporary passion in Europe, the vacant point around which ideals clash. Easily available as a token, existing everywhere and nowhere, he is talked about constantly. But in the current public conversation, this figure has not only migrated from one country to another, he has migrated from reality to the collective imagination where he has been transformed into a terrible fiction.

Whether he or she – and I will call the immigrant he, while being aware that he is stripped of colour, gender and character – the immigrant has been made into something resembling an alien. He is an example of the undead, who will invade, colonise and contaminate, a figure we can never quite digest or vomit. If the twentieth century was replete with uncanny, semi-fictional figures who invaded the decent, upright and hard-working – the pure – this character is re-haunting us in the guise of the immigrant. He is both a familiar insidious figure, and a new edition of an old idea expressed with refreshed and forceful rhetoric.

Unlike other monsters, the foreign body of the immigrant is unslayable. Resembling a zombie in a video game, he is impossible to kill or finally eliminate not only because he is already silent and dead, but also because there are waves of other similar immigrants just over the border coming right at you. Forgetting that it is unworkable notions of the 'normal' – the fascist normal – which make the usual seem weird, we like to believe that there was a better time when the world didn't shift so much and everything appeared more permanent. We were all alike and comprehensible to one another, and these spectres didn't forever seethe at the windows. Now there seems to be general agreement that all this global movement could be a catastrophe, since these omnivorous figures will eat us alive. From this point of view, the immigrant is eternal: unless we act, he will forever be a source of contagion and horror.

It is impossible to speak up for the immigrant or, more importantly, hear him speak for himself, since everyone, including the most reasonable and sensitive, has made up their mind that the immigrant is everywhere now, and he is too much of a problem. There is, of course, always good reason to be suspicious of agreement: there is nothing more coercive and stupid than consensus, and it is through consensus that inequality is concealed.

Nevertheless, the immigrant is easily dismissed and denigrated since he is now no longer a person. The recently arrived immigrant, the last through the door, and now settling down in the new country, can himself be disgusted by the idea of this newer arrival or interloper, the one who could take his place, because this threatening Other does not resemble him in any way. The migrant has no face, no status, no protection and no story. His single identity is to be discussed within the limited rules of the community.

Too superstitious, ambitious, worthless and strange – deposited outside the firmament of the acceptable – the migrant is degraded to the status of an object about whom anything can be said and to whom anything can be done. One thing is certain about him: he will not only rob you of your wealth and social position, he will be monstrous and obscene in his pleasures. These jouissances, it goes without saying, he has obtained at your expense, even as he is subjugated as your slave.

As an idea, then, this concept of the immigrant is familiar, and the usual clichés – the confining power of negative description – apply, as they always have done to those shadows who haunt the in-between or border zones. The immigrant will be in-bred, suffer from sexual incontinence and mental illness and will be both needy and greedy. But in this particular form the immigrant is also a relatively recent creation. Since we depend so much on that which we hate the most, the worse the economy the more the need for the immigrant – even in a time when we like to compliment ourselves on our relative tolerance.

Women, gays, the disabled and other former marginals might, after some struggle, have been afforded dignity, a voice and a place. Yet diversity and multiculturalism can become forms of exoticism and self-idealisation, and exaggerations of difference new types of conceit. Meanwhile, a necessary level of hatred is kept going with regard to the reviled figure of the immigrant. Integration can never continue; there has to be someone shoved off the map. Today it will be him, and tomorrow someone else: the circulation of bodies is determined by profit. The rich buy freedom; they can always go where they like while the poor are not welcome anywhere. But, all the time, by some perverse magical alchemy, those we need, exploit and persecute the most are turned into our persecutors.

Others only have the power we give them. The immigrant is a collective hallucination forged in our own minds. This ever developing notion, like God or the devil, is an important creation, being part of ourselves, but the paranoiac, looking wildly around, can never see that the foreign body is inside him. Of course not: when the world is divided so definitively into the Hollywood binaries of good and bad, no one can think clearly. Hate skews reality even more than love. If the limits of the world are made by language, we need better words for all this. The idea of the immigrant creates anxiety only because he is unknown and has to be kept that way.

This group fantasy and prison of cliché – a base use of the imagination – reduces the world to a gothic tale where there is only the violence of exclusion, and nothing can be thought or done. If it could be, the stranger, with a mixture of naivety and knowing, might be in a position to tell us the truth about ourselves, since he sees more than we know.

Amanda Craig
METAMORPHOSIS 2

One morning Katie F woke from restless dreams to find herself transformed into a gigantic cockroach. She lay on her back, and wondered what was going on. Although her body was still a bright orange colour, it was now quite hard and shiny, with two bands near the abdomen. Her many legs, thin as wires compared to the rest of her, waved feebly as she looked.

'What's happened to me?' she thought.

It wasn't a dream. Her room, a proper human room, was just as it had always been. A collection of newspapers lay spread out on the table – for Katie F was a celebrity – and above it was a magazine portrait that she had framed in a pretty gilded frame, showing a woman with dyed blonde hair, blue eyes, a big pearl necklace and large white teeth smiling at the viewer in a way that was neither friendly nor inviting. This was Katie F herself, and she was proud of it.

'Got to get up,' she said to herself. Her body was not well adapted to standing upright, but she had two daughters to take to school, and couldn't lie around. It was a very expensive school, where all the girls had nice names like Arabella and Letitia, and were so respectful of teachers that they stood frozen against the corridor walls when one passed by, never raising their eyes.

'Perhaps they won't notice my looking like this,' she thought. 'After all, I am their mother.'

It was easy to throw off the duvet, because it was made from goose feathers, but harder to roll over. She lay there, waving her little legs quite helplessly for a while, and contracting her abdomen just as she had learned to do in the zumba class until, somehow, she slid off the bed and landed quite hard on the floor. It hurt, but there was no gain without pain, and now she was onto her many feet it was all systems go. Good heavens, was that the time? With an effort to stand on her back legs, Katie F made her way to the wardrobe where her clothes were. It was challenging to get the door open, but she did, and then she began squeezing her hard orange body into her usual top-range designer outfit for the school run.

In the end, she managed it all quite well, thanks to some enormous dark glasses, headphones and bright pink lipstick, although she had no shoes for her six feet and her long antennae had to be kept back with a headband. She got out cereal and milk, but was unable to eat any herself, because cockroaches dislike milk. Her daughters were so good that they ate all their breakfast without looking up once from their plates, and didn't notice when Katie F suddenly plunged her head in the rubbish bin and ate up all the left-over food there. It was strange behaviour from a respectable middle-class person like herself, but when she finished, she felt very pleased because she had made sure that nothing had been wasted, which was more than could be said for the people who got disgustingly fat on fast food.

Getting the car going was easier than expected, too. It had power steering that responded to the touch of Katie F's little legs, and she was able to open it electronically with a touch of her antennae. She liked the feeling of being in a darker, more enclosed space, and it didn't matter that once or twice she nearly knocked over a cyclist on the road, as her car was built like a tank. All she had to do was to pull up on the zig-zag yellow lines and drop the girls off.

'Great tan!' called another mother. 'Is that coat Prada?'

Katie F nodded. Nobody noticed anything different about her, which proved that all you needed to succeed was confidence.

As soon as she got home, her mobile started ringing. It was a newspaper, wanting to hear her views on the refugee crisis.

'There isn't a refugee crisis, there's an economic migrant crisis,' Katie F said.

'I can't hear you too well,' said the editor.

Her voice sounded strangely full of crackles and hissing, but she blamed it on a poor connection.

'Who cares if they starve? There are millions of them swarming over here, we can't be soft on them. They should stay in their own country. My antennae tell me that the British people won't stand for this kind of nonsense.'

Her antennae were, in fact, waving about because Katie F's cleaner had just walked in. No sooner did she see her employer than she let out a piercing shriek.

'It's me,' said Katie F, but the cleaner only shouted a stream of imprecations in Kosovan, and waved her hoover nozzle threateningly.

'Filthy bug! Devil! Get out or I kill you.'

Katie F hissed, but then instinct took over. She scuttled out of the door, and into the street.

Outside on the cold grey pavement, she met with no better reception. People failed to notice her, or if they did, drew away from her sharply, or shouted abuse. It was nothing she hadn't handled already when going into TV studios to air her views, and Katie F hissed at them all. How revolting they were! Couldn't they see that she was a celebrity, and if she just happened to have turned into a giant cockroach then it wasn't as if she were fat, or tattooed or a foreigner. But that was the problem with the British public, whatever you gave them they would always moan.

It was no wonder that so many of them were unemployed with an attitude like that.

From time to time, ordinary people still recognised her and exclaimed, 'Aren't you Katie F?'

Some of them would ask for her autograph, but then they'd realise that they were talking to a gigantic cockroach and they would run away, screaming,

Being a full-time mother who never made a fuss about it, Katie F lingered near her home for a while, checking up on her daughters. They were being looked after by their useless father, pulling his weight at last, but Katie F used her initiative and went off to look for something better. That was what was wrong with human beings, they didn't have the slightest idea what to do with their lives and spent half their time sleeping, whereas cockroaches were always busy eating or cleaning their antennae or making more cockroaches. Over the next few days, despite her energetic recycling of lazy humans' waste, she began to shrink – result! As if anyone needed to be a plus-sized bug, when a little discipline made it much easier to slip into pubs, dustbins and houses. Initially, she stuck to streets like her own, but soon found a flat where immigrants were sleeping six to a room, the floor a sea of mattresses, a dead giveaway that they were illegal and on benefits. They were still picky, though, because if one of them saw her they'd scream and try to bash her with a boot.

'Piss off, I'm British!' she hissed, but their English wasn't good enough to understand even the simplest words.

'Dirty, dirty!' they cried. It was the only word they knew, apart from 'police', and 'help'. They made no effort to integrate, and some wouldn't even leave, sitting there like great big cry-babies, sighing and moaning. Look at me, she wanted to say: I've been turned into a giant cockroach but I'm not complaining, am I? They might have backs and arms and legs ridged and pocked with scars and burns, but what was the fuss about? Why couldn't they just toughen up and grow a thicker skin, like Katie F?

Yet the climate made her restive. As the year was drained of its warmth, she began to look for heat but every day was a little colder. Eventually, Katie F spotted an empty lorry, returning to Europe. It was a matter of moments to scuttle onto it because of course nobody wanted to leave Britain, only to get there. By now she was so much smaller that her little legs carried her faster than ever, and she clung on, or rolled around like an amber bead on the floor. The empty lorry rumbled onto a ferry and off again, and then they were passing a jumble of plastic tents and cardboard sheets and rubbish heaps where people squatted or stood about holding placards, or else made sudden dashes to get over and under the barbed wire fences. They were too big to avoid capture, being stupid lumbering humans, and the other humans didn't think to spray them with poison as they did cockroaches. There weren't many pickings to be had there, though, and it was too cold, so she waited for another lorry, and moved on South because that was where her antennae told her she'd find heat.

Soon her path was crossing with those travelling in the opposite direction. She passed wave after wave of humans, tramping along through the countryside in an endless file, all the idiots who had brought their kids, their grannies, their disabled, to push or pull in buggies and carts and wheelchairs or carry on their shoulders, their soft human bodies getting slower and wearier and colder and more bruised. By contrast Katie F's hard little body was working with increased efficiency and speed the warmer it became. She wasn't weak and slow like people: as a cockroach she could live for a month without food.

The warmer it became, the harder her little legs worked. Within days, she reached the sea, and there, too, was more rubbish floating about, including several humans who had drowned. Katie F hissed to herself in disgust. Her excellent many-lensed eyes soon showed her where an empty rubber dinghy was floating on the shore, as if waiting to convey her. She scuttled onto it, and soon the dinghy was being driven across the sea by the wind. The waves were whipped into walls of water that swelled to the size of houses and yet there were still humans coming in the opposite direction, huddled together like greedy fools. She could see them clutching each other, screaming, trying to keep their children from capsizing, sinking, drowning. Why did these idiots fling themselves into the water if they couldn't swim?

At last the deflating dinghy landed on a shore, and her hard little body quivered with the heat. This was more like it! She ran up the beach and along a dusty road until she came to a place that was all broken concrete and twisted metal and craters. Here, at last, humans were running from place to place, shooting at each other, crawling on their abdomens into ragged tunnels and dark places where the noise and tremors from explosions had them all shaking. Only they could never run as fast as she could, having only two legs and a foolish tendency to bleed when cut. There were not many humans left, and indeed Katie F soon discovered that they had been replaced by far more of her own kind, and that the entire city as it was emptied was now filling with the tough, armoured bodies of cockroaches. What a wonderful place this was! The cockroaches swarmed over more and more, and when fire fell from the sky it simply gave them more to eat. They would survive anything, anywhere, and the world was theirs as it always had been.

'How much better it is to be as I am,' Katie F said to herself, running about in her new home.

For cockroaches can live for a whole week with their heads blown off.

Stephen Kelman

SELFIE

I see him from a distance and I know what he is, and I think about crossing the street so I won't have to refuse him. But there are cars in the way and other people and I can't find a gap, so I keep going and hope that when I'm near enough to hear him his words will fail or someone else will take the hit for me, a kinder soul than mine or one in need of his goods. His goods. You can get them anywhere, on every street from a thousand men just like him. They're all the same, only the colours change.

The men who sell them, their colours don't change. Every one of them is brown, a deep brown of coffee grounds at the bottom of the cup, in this city of espresso and holstered cops who look the other way. But this man has seen me. It's too late to busy myself in the act of ignoring him, to window-shop or kneel to tie a shoelace. I'm wearing slip-ons and this is summer in Rome, and on this shopping street he is one of many and I have said 'No thank you' so many times before that I've stopped feeling the words on their way out. I could be anyone else and the response would be the same. And he's the same as the others, and he expects no different from me, and so his eyes are tired but yet he wills something hopeful from them and he asks me anyway.

'Selfie?' is his question. One word and yet he fills it with so much, and yet it means nothing at all. And perhaps he's aware of the futility of the word and perhaps he's not. And I stop and look at what he's holding.

'Selfie?' he says again, and he shows me the thing in his hand as an aid to my understanding.

I don't need a selfie stick, his or anybody else's. I take my pictures the old-fashioned way, with a camera you can't make calls on, and I believe some moments are best recorded minus the intrusion of my own face. Such a moment follows when I glance down at the street for anonymity and see his brown toes peeking out of plastic thongs, the two toes on his left foot rubbing up against each other like infants holding on to each other through a storm at sea in a boat made of tyres, and I wonder if anybody loved this man and told him so before he left. It would seem such a long way to come without love. Or perhaps he hoped to find it here.

I look him in the eyes then, and he shrinks from me. I should have said 'No thank you' by now and moved on. That I still stand in front of him leaves him perplexed and he backs away one step and peers beyond me, looking for another soul to whisper his pitch to, yearning to be ignored again because to be ignored means he has arrived, he is one among many and they all look the same.

I would like to tell him that I envy his toes, because they're brown and hairless and more suited to the fresh air than mine. I would like to say that being white is not all it's cracked up to be. But I doubt his English would stretch to an appreciation of well-meaning irony. I doubt he would see the kindness in me, in my tourist hat and my patterned shirt, the hair on my arms matted in SPF 50 and the ring on my finger denoting a wife somewhere who cares to know that I'm fed and to where I travel when I dream. I should keep this simple.

To give him hope, I look at the things he's holding again. He's holding them tightly as if they were charms against bad weather. He has many, so has sold few. If only I needed what he is offering me. If only I could pretend I needed them – but then wouldn't that be a kindness too far, wouldn't that unman him?

'Good price,' he says, and he opens out a sample to show me how it works. It's telescopic for capturing the background details. I saw them at the Coliseum and at the Spanish Steps, I saw them outside my hotel and on the Piazza Navona and I wondered then what kind of background needed me in its way. And now I am in his way. He has a living to make and I'm holding him up. I should say it in a way he will understand, so that he doesn't doubt my intentions.

Other people are coming between us and outside one shop an old man in a morning suit dances for money, and he is white and from here so his need is not so great.

'Where are you from?' I ask.

'Selfie,' the man replies, and somehow I know it will be the last familiar word he says to me. His skin is built for this weather and they all look the same, and nobody stops to talk to them because nobody knows what to say. I would like to be the one who knows. I would like to be kind in a way he will understand.

'I don't need one, look,' I say, and I show him my camera. 'Have you sold many today?'

Kindness is so naked without the words to clothe it, and nobody likes to look at a naked man. Out here on the street. In the summer. When there's shopping to be done and gelatos to be eaten – this girl here holds one the size of a topiary and it's drip-dripping down her arm and all these men must look the same to her, so fresh and so unbitten is she by the teeth of time. She doesn't see them but I have. I have seen you now and I don't want to go away without you knowing that I'm not the same as the others.

Is there a part of the city where you can be with others like you, where you eat and talk and lend and borrow money? Where do you live and what fills the hours when you're not here on this street? Is it just washing clothes and sleeping and phone calls to loved ones back across the water and the endless land, or is there also time to laugh and be drunken and loud? What is your background and which of its details do you take to bed with you as balms against indigenous spores? Are you ever happy as I am?

I can't say any of this, I don't possess the words. If only a look was enough. My eyes bear my kindness but you won't look at them. I look just like everyone else to you.

Would it be all right if I touched you? Just my hand on yours to show that we're the same. I was in India once and I was in New York, and there are people everywhere who would like to be touched if only the offer were made. You don't have to if you don't want. It just seems a shame not to touch if the chance comes along.

And then he's talking in his own language, and it's about me but not to me, for he is looking past me and above me and anywhere but at me, and I won't get out of his way.

Should I be sorry for holding him up? He doesn't have to be anywhere. This spot is his world and if he moves from it everything comes crashing down. Someone will buy one soon, but they're not lining up right now. He doesn't look hungry and he doesn't look scared, he just looks tired and in need of a hand on his. But it can't be mine. We're not the same.

If I had to sell selfie sticks on the street I would go insane. Nobody has ever bought one as far as I can tell, but they keep coming back every day. They have to carry them around with them from where they live to where they work. I get the feeling those two places are very far apart and the sun is beating down, and at least your skin is built for this, you'll never burn I suppose or stop coming here. Why is nobody buying? Don't they know how far you've come to be here? People just don't know, and I'm not like them. If only you had something I needed.

The old man is finished dancing and he holds out a hat and people walk away. He might have been loved before and he might still be. There should be a law against that kind of thing, people shouldn't have to dance for money. I notice that my hand has become lodged in my pocket and I slide it out. My wallet is in there and the leather is sweating through the fabric of my trousers. Still the brown man is talking past me and his words are quick and fraught like the beating of tar-dipped wings and then they stop.

Another person walks past him without looking at his face, but I have seen his face now and I want never to forget it. My money can stay where it is, his need of it can't be so great if he has clothes and his belly is bigger than mine.

On the news they all escaped the same mudslide or marketplace bomb, they all come over together in boxes in the same freight train or curled around the axles of the same long haulage truck. They were stuck together through the worst nature could throw at them and through the lowliest ideals of evacuation. When they make land they must scatter as insects do under torch beams. They must behave as insects do to preserve what makes them human in the glare of the law. I don't want him to be alone any more. There must be somewhere he goes after where he can be with others like him. So many of them in the city, they all have toes like his. Better suited to the weather. At night they gather in, it's the only thing that makes sense. He's never alone for long, only in the days.

At the Pantheon too and in front of the Trevi Fountain all scaffolded and curtained off, and nobody was buying because they all look the same. People need a distinguishing feature. If one had a longer handle or there was something different in the design, that might draw people in. Everyone who needed one had one already, I never saw any money change hands. I like to keep out of my pictures, it's the background that interests me.

I decide as his eyelids droop and he forgets my presence that he is loved and missed in the way of a breadwinner. I decide that he has a name that would tingle my lips like music, and that his name means something to those who bestowed it. It's taken from the land he was born into, it describes his bond with the seasons and topography of the valley or the plain or the street from where he rose. In India I saw children like his who worked the hotel drive-ups pressing flowers into tourists' palms for rice and milk. With his darkness he could be Bangladeshi but I decide he is from the India I visited with my camera and my notebook. I sketched his children's likenesses and snapped them when they weren't looking. I bought their pinwheels on Chowpatty beach and dropped notes into their hands at teeming intersections where the stop lights allowed for the exchange of dusters for small money imprinted with the smell of skin and earth. They all looked the same and I remarked to myself that I loved them all equally until the lights changed. I decide that he is a father to them and a son of rape in the alleys of a slum that I saw recreated on a West End stage. I decide that we would have been friends if I were brown like him and came from the same place. We would have bickered over bottles in the squatting sun and whistled at the same girls, their limbs springy and unrooted as fawns to deliver them from our enlusting gaze.

I decide that he couldn't make it in my country with the cold and the politics, that he needs sunlight year-round and the shoppers to keep him afloat. They are the sea he is expediently lost in and we all look the same to him. I decide he sends money home not just for rice and milk, but to build a library on the banks of an open sewer so that children like his own can climb its books up to the stars. I decide he is a dissident and his escape was from the clutches of the ringmasters he caricatured with sharp and noble slogans. The only reason we can't be the same is because we lack the words. Our uncommon languages are what keep us hidden from each other. Only words sever us.

He wipes his eyes and he might have been crying or it might have been the blossoms of the Roman summer that fly at our faces and flare our nostrils to the suspension of a sneeze that won't come. I want to hear him sneeze so that I can compare the noise it makes to mine. I want to tell him that I understand him on the level of involuntary reactions to airborne irritants. I want to tell him that in this minute of watching I have found the truth of us. It's a truth he would appreciate if his words and mine were in sympathy. The truth is this: we're both in it for the money.

The secret I keep from him is this: I paid ten euros for a muffin at a café with a famous name and a literary history. I couldn't tell him even if our words were equal, because it would hurt him and me both to admit to it. He's worth more than a muffin. But he is not what I wanted, and I've worked hard to have the little things.

'Selfie, selfie.'

He prods his stick towards another tourist who grabs its end and pushes back at him. He stumbles and almost loses his footing. He stands straight again and the tourist is already gone to part rows of tourist T-shirts as if they were trees in a magical forest.

I look at the man and purse my lips in apology for the rudeness of others, and I know that I can't help him because I have no need of what he offers. My camera, see? I raise it and point it at him. There is a slight flinch from him but he stands up to it. I square my shot and hold the button down to focus and press it to fire and I capture him in a moment of poise. He is strong and courageous and I show him the image. He doesn't smile at it. I don't delete it. It's my souvenir of him. The background is blurred so that the central subject can be more sharply realised. My camera has a setting for this.

I think about a handshake but his hands are full with the things he is selling. They all look the same and I want him to be lucky. There is gelato down the street in so many flavours and before I leave I will try every one.

Ruth Padel

Excerpts from

CHILDREN OF STORM

The new garden is an empty yard paved in pink and yellow stone. We've cut down some Leylandii taking all the light and there are no trees. I've seen a wren once, and two goldfinches. But it's July, birds will be finding food elsewhere, we'll have to wait till we plant grass, bushes, trees. My daughter has fitted her stuff into her tiny new room and left for work in Colombia, and there's a lot to do to turn this into a home. But we love it; these back gardens now seem normal.

But they're not normal – not in the age of migration with billions of people moving unhoused across the globe.

A robin, once he's won his territory, fiercely defends it against other robins, often to the death. So do we. In every country, earlier immigrants resent new ones and try to keep them out.

From the beginning of mass migrations to America in the 1880s, there were calls for restrictions, and immigration laws. The Chinese Exclusion Act, Alien Contract Labor Law, Quota Laws, National Origins Act.

Twenty years ago, when my daughter was small, I lived in Greece when Albanian immigrants were a new phenomenon. The same Albanians are now the naturalised fathers of boys persecuting Pakistani and Somali immigrants to keep Greece, they say, for the Greeks.

Asylum means 'the place which can't be plundered'. It was a sacred concept in archaic Greece. At an altar, you were safe. You were a recognised suppliant, you had crossed into sacred space. Anyone who violated asylum was accursed. But the first reliably dated event in the history of Athens, a hundred or so years before democracy began, was the betrayal of asylum.

In 632 BC, an Athenian nobleman named Cylon attempted a coup d'état at Athens. He captured the Acropolis but was besieged there and took asylum in the Temple of Athena. He escaped; the rulers persuaded his less fortunate supporters to leave asylum and stand trial. They promised to spare their lives but the suppliants were rightly wary and tied a rope to the goddess's statue as they came out to maintain asylum. The rope broke, or was cut, and the rulers claimed the goddess had repudiated her suppliants. The suppliants were stoned to death but the rulers had violated the law against killing suppliants and their clan was cursed. This curse was still significant two hundred years later in the democracy, and could be used politically against their descendants. Asylum was a political issue before democracy began and has remained so ever since.

In the UK, a stamp saying LOC, for Lack of Credibility, has appeared on files as a reason to refuse asylum. One small mistake in any part of your statement is a reason to disbelieve all your testimony. Applicants are held in detention centres while a decision is made either to let them stay or to deport them to the country they came from.

The UK has thirteen detention centres, whose title was formally changed in 2002 to Immigration Removal Centres. Some of these are run by private companies contracted by the government. They are for people seeking asylum, or people thought to be illegal immigrants. Asylum seekers are put in them when they arrive and held while waiting for their case to be decided, or waiting to be deported when it has been refused. The conditions of these centres have been criticised by the UK Inspector of Prisons and a report by the Medical Foundation for the Care of Victims of Torture (now Freedom from Torture) and Medical Justice speaks of 'systematic abuse' within them; of hunger strikes, riots, suicides, complaints of rape, assault, intimidation, and lack of information about your basic rights.

People will do anything to keep out of them. In 2004, twenty-three Chinese migrant workers died in the mudflats of Morecambe Bay. Nick Broomfield's film *Ghosts* recreated their story. Having paid Snakehead gangs to smuggle them on a year-long journey across Asia and Europe, they were put to agricultural labour, and then to cockling, by gangmasters. Just as *The Aeneid* ends with indigenous Italians making war on the Trojan refugees, they were beaten up by British rivals who took their cockle-sacks. So they picked cockles at night, stuck in the mud as the tide came in, and drowned.

Migration is a lottery. Thousands of migrating animals and people die; thousands find the conditions in the new place very tough. But for humans there are still further psychological costs. A friend of mine, a psychiatrist for the homeless, was called out recently in the night because one of his patients, a Muonyjang from South Sudan, suddenly had to be hospitalised.

Several years after coming to Britain, this man and his mother were reunited with his elder brother. All three escaped massacre in South Sudan when the boys were eight and five. To give the family more chance of surviving they decided to split up. The elder boy was recruited as a child soldier. He saw and did unspeakable things but eventually escaped, was rescued in Ethiopia by the UN, and is now a successful businessman.

The mother went with the younger son to Egypt; they reached Britain, he grew up and went to a British university but suddenly broke down and wound up homeless on the London streets.

Migration may bring new life. But the loss of the home and the traumas you endured, the reason you had to flee in the first place, may also take their toll long after, in breakdown.

Turn the crystal of 'migration' and you get 'home'. It is the Home Office that deals with immigration – and detention – in Britain. It also manages deportation. In the mid-1990s, the Home Office began what medical agencies call outsourcing abuse: hiring private companies to take home refused asylum seekers.

This is a new industry. The companies are called escort agencies or security solutions firms. Reports by charities have found multiple abuses in deportation. The escorts are on hourly pay and have a financial incentive but don't get a bonus unless they return the deportees to their country of origin. A record of criminal assault is no bar to employment as an escort and their actions are not open to public scrutiny.

In 2010 at Heathrow, three escorts from an international security solutions firm called G4S boarded a plane for Luanda with an Angolan man, Jimmy Mubenga. Passengers heard Mubenga shouting that he didn't want to leave his wife and children; and that he couldn't breathe. His last words were, 'They're trying to kill me.' The aircraft returned to the terminal; he was pronounced dead in hospital. Escorts are allowed to use control techniques approved by the Prison Service. Pushing a deportee's head between his legs, however, is forbidden. Death from it is called positional asphyxia.

Postscript: I wrote this piece, and the following poems, five years ago before Syria exploded, when the main route of migration into Greece was over land. As the world sees every day on TV, this situation has now changed beyond any bad dream imaginable in 2011. Every day, hundreds of thousands of refugees are scrambling out (if they survive) of overloaded dinghies onto rocky shores of small islands, sometimes very remote islands, whose fragile infrastructures cannot help and cannot cope. Generous individuals do what they can. But the figure in 'Oresteiada' who bought a 'post-Soviet My Little Pony' from an Albanian immigrant in Athens twenty-five years ago is currently on Lesbos, watching despairing Greek officials lock up refugees. 'But,' as 'Oresteiada' says, 'they keep coming.'

Ruth Padel, Easter 2016

GHOST SHIP

You have to get out. But this is how you imagine
you might go, when you wake at night afraid
of moving on from Gambia or Guinea Bissau

and hear the redslick in your temple beat
like waves around the ghost ship
discovered off Ragged Point, Barbados.

A six-foot yacht, adrift. No name, no flag
and a phantom crew, eleven young men
in green, red, orange, blue,

mummified in salt of their own sweat.
You can't shake out of your head
that airline ticket from Senegal, the note

in a dead boy's pocket – *Excuse me, this is the end,*
sorry to my family in Bassada –
saying how the skipper
disappeared before they left Cape Verde;

how he could have jumped like his friend,
when they were towed; and how one night
the rope was slashed by a machete.

ORESTIADA

Any weakening in Fortress Europe shows
In ripples of the icy Hebros
still carrying a memory
of the floating head of Orpheus.
Twenty years ago, the novelty
was Immigrant Market at Theseion:

Albanians, squatting on unravelled
plastic tartan, offering cut-price replicas
of everything under the sun.
You invested, Kerin, in a present
for your god-daughter: a cochineal
post-Soviet My Little Pony.

In Athens today, you see *No Mosques*
and *This is Greece* sprayed over the square
as Albanian vigilantes chase the Afghans out.
People-traffickers from Troy
throw their customers in the Hebros
and asphyxiate stowaways in trucks.

But they keep coming, over a forest frontier
of landmines and razor wire,
carrying toddlers and plastic bags
to hide behind a furniture factory
in suburbs of Orestiada, the city named
for the boy who knifed his mother and went mad.

THE PLACE WITHOUT A DOOR

Listen. There are dragons under cities
and monsters in white spaces on sea maps.
Sangatte is a commune on the coast of France
facing water which the English call English Channel.
A border for which many men, and women too,
have died. The name is Gap-in-Sand.
When we were there, we knew
it was the Place Without a Door.
Mark the spot in my brother's heart
where he built a cardboard shrine
for our wasteland jungle. Check the wall
where someone graffed, *Nous voulons de l'air*
pour nos enfants. The cement octagons
where we hid at night to rush the axle
of Spanish lorries. The bridge where my brother
jumped that train into the tunnel.

Moris Farhi

CLOUD-DERVISH

I met my Guide – known to many who trod mystic latitudes in those days as 'Bulut-Derviş', 'Cloud-Dervish' – in İstanbul soon after my thirteenth birthday.

I was a disturbed boy then. Pretentious as it sounds, I was in search of God.

My syndrome, consensually agreed by the swarm of psychoanalysts, assigned to buzz around me as if I were their queen bee, was the common but specious *mal du siècle* of the young – though in my case, these experts, baffled like most sophists by the mind's propensity for constructing Daedalean mazes, pontificated that my disorder, patently incubated by my dysfunctional parents, was not specious but genuine, indeed inevitable.

True, my parents were traumatised; but, blessed with Milky Ways of love with which they embraced people, never dysfunctional! Their traumas were simply the perdurable Furies that plague most survivors. Thus, my mother – a Greek-Jewess from Salonika – would constantly send her soul to search the soot of Auschwitz's crematoria for sparks that would convince her that the father, sister and other family members, even while vested in smoke, had migrated to a parallel world where Holocausts were unknown. Thus also my father – a Turkish-Jew from İzmir – having eluded Death, when still in his teens, in the great fire that devastated the city in 1922, would toil steadfastly as a

Samaritan in the Talmudic belief that saving even one life might save the world.

That said, I should admit that, as I witnessed my parents' valiant efforts to alchemise Evil into Good, my derangement suppurated. I lost faith in God. Indicting Him of indifference to barbarity, I stopped searching for Him. I even refused to perform my bar mitzvah, the coming-of-age ritual that every Jewish boy must undergo to become a 'son of the commandment'.

My father, mortified by my aberration and fearful that it might constrain the Rabbinate to issue the censuring *herem* that would expel me from Jewish society, decided to seek a healer beyond the psychoanalytic pool.

Eventually, on the recommendation of a nonagenarian Kabbalist, he took me to a Sufi *Murshid* who spread out his prayer-mat for stray individuals every Friday morning in the picnic-site by the Rumeli Fortress.

My father's choice of a Muslim ascetic instead of a Jewish sage, though most unorthodox, was, in effect, astute. Sufism is the only sect within the three monotheisms that keeps its doors open to everybody, especially to wanderers, idolaters and the generally misguided. But what, above all, convinced my father was that the *Murshid*, originally from a Mevlevi Order, pursued a nonconformist mysticism that many traditionalist Sufis considered as schismatic – this despite the fact that to achieve Sufism's ultimate aim, union with The Godhead, the adherent must traverse the infinite mysticities dictated by the soul. Consequently, with true Judaic liberalism, my father saw the *Murshid* as a new-age Spinoza, the philosopher ostracised by Dutch Jews.

I did not readily consent to my father's proposition. I had friends who lived in the vicinity of the Rumeli Fortress and asked them to appraise the Sufi.

They reported that he was an Ahıska Turk born as İbrahim Raşid, in Georgia, then still a Soviet Socialist

Republic. When, in 1944, haunted by the threat that Germany might open a new front against the USSR, Stalin, in order to clear the Caucasus of Turkish sympathisers, had deported most of the Ahıska to Central Asia, the Raşids had somehow avoided the expulsion. After the Second World War and particularly during the nascence of the independent Georgian Republic, ethnic and religious prejudices against the Ahıska had escalated. Sometime in the mid-1990s, the Raşids had chosen to emigrate. The family, preferring to stay in the Caucasus, had moved to Dagestan while İbrahim, longing to imbibe the air breathed by the great Sufi Master, Mevlânâ Celâleddin-i Rumi, had slipped into Turkey.

He was middle-aged and lived in the storeroom of the local grocery store where he worked as a night-watchman. Much loved and respected, everybody – even his employer – called him 'Cloud-Dervish'. (As he revealed later, he had stoically accepted the sobriquet even though it infringed his belief that birth-names mapped the hidden paths of one's journey through life.)

The sobriquet – in my view more of an epithet like 'Law-giver' for Moses and Sultan Süleyman – was an apt one. It had been conferred on him for his disposition to assign, in his parables, specific objectives to clouds. Clouds, he maintained, were God's runes. By limning the past, the present and the future, they endowed humanity with roots, continuum, knowledge, culture and art. (One narrative that became popular related how a particular cluster of clouds depicted Marco Polo's journey to China where, observing silkworms feasting on mulberry leaves, he took a cutting from a mulberry tree and thus launched the European silk industry.)

Not surprisingly, every detail of this scant information – particularly the fact that his epithet struck me as felicitously poetic – prompted me to meet him.

And so one Friday morning, my father took me to the picnic-site by the Rumeli Fortress.

We found Cloud-Dervish whirling with some of his followers on a grassy patch overlooking the Bosporus. (The followers are known as *murids*, that gossamer Arabic word that means 'desirous' of God's Love and defines the person who endeavours to ascend to The Divine Presence by purifying his inner self.)

As Cloud-Dervish whirled I felt transported to a becalmed shore. I can only describe the abandon – so surprisingly precise – of his turns, the way he moulded the aether into luminosity, as the salvational realm we crave in our darkest hours. Those who have glimpsed flashes of light in hurricanes will understand my entrancement.

After the whirling, Cloud-Dervish and the *murids* sat around his prayer-mat and meditated.

We waited for the *murids* to leave.

Finally, in mid-afternoon, he beckoned us.

He scrutinised me a moment then turned to my father. 'The boy is a lost soul. As we all are. But God sees him and knows his heart. Leave him with me.'

His voice was like an embrace – both gentle and strong.

My father thanked him and left.

Cloud-Dervish riveted his eyes on me. 'Sit.'

I sat across from him and tried to hold his gaze. His turquoise eyes changed hues in tune with the light and the breeze. They reminded me of the mythical Persian gemstone that, when effulgent, protected a person from unnatural death and, when dusky, forewarned doom.

Eventually, he smiled. 'You and your father waited patiently. He because he loves you. You because you seek the Truth. You will probably never see The Godhead. But I believe you will try.'

I nodded.

He pointed at his prayer-mat, which was multi-coloured

and depicted clouds of every shape. 'They indicate the paths to The Divine Presence. Which are innumerable. These are only those I can detect.'

To my surprise I understood what he meant without understanding the paths' courses. (Later, I would discover that, despite their innumerability, the paths had only one destination: the union with The Godhead at the unseen centre of the Ultimate Truth. But I also discovered that no matter how well one progressed on one's chosen path, only the very few completed the journey and attained Oneness with The Godhead.)

He offered me a sherbet. 'It's sundown. When all beverages suffuse the mind with radiance. This is my own blend – spiked with herbs gathered on my wanderings.'

I drank it. It tasted like nectar.

'Now meditate.'

'How?'

'Find a path.'

I looked up at the sky and tried to pick a cloud to conjure Marco Polo and his mulberry cutting.

I fell asleep.

I didn't conjure Marco Polo. Instead I dreamt about concentration camps, deportations of minorities and the genocides that were happening everywhere in the world.

When I woke up it was dark.

Cloud-Dervish was still there, watching me. 'You're haunted by our world – a good sign.'

I nodded, wondering how he had penetrated my dream.

He rolled up his prayer-mat and rose. 'Slaughter and deracination – history summed up. They haunt me, too.'

I muttered. 'But you can escape all that. You can turn to God.'

'Turning to God means repairing hearts – as many as humanly possible.' He ruffled my hair. 'If you want to meet again, I'll be here.'

And so I became one of Cloud-Dervish's *murids*. (I should confess: sensitive to the importance he attached to birth-names, I called him İbrahim, but in my soul he was – and will always be – Cloud-Dervish.)

I engaged in *dhikr*, that devotional act that induces awareness of The Divine Presence by repeating His various explicative names. I danced, whirled and recited adulatory poems in *sema* ceremonies. I endeavoured to withdraw from mundane preoccupations by surrendering myself to *muraqaba*, the meditation that attunes one to The Godhead.

Except for my parents, the community decided that by immersing myself in Sufism I had renounced my Judaism. Actually, the opposite was true. Sufism invigorated my Judaism and affirmed its vessels of morality which harbour righteousness, compassion, altruism, justice and equality; above all, it reminded me that since Evil relentlessly damages these life-sustaining vessels every Jew is commanded to repair them assiduously.

I should also stress that Cloud-Dervish, in true Sufi spirit, sanctioned his non-Muslim followers to address God by any name they preferred instead of Allah as tradition demanded. In fact, when addressing his Jewish followers – yes, I had persuaded a few friends to join us – he revealed how Sufism had influenced the Jews of Moorish Spain, and how Jewish scholars of those times had charted the ascetic paths wherein their co-religionists could communicate with God by perceiving both the visible and the invisible. (Profoundly affected by this disclosure, I called God not by His Jewish appellation but, inspired by the great Sufi poet Yunus Emre, as 'The Beloved'.)

I should also admit that I did eventually perform my bar mitzvah. I did so on Cloud-Dervish's counsel that the ritual, mystical in its own way, would elevate me to adulthood, make me accountable for all my actions and relieve my parents from all the wrongdoings I was bound to commit.

Seven years later, one pristine winter day when thick snow muted Nature – for Cloud-Dervish an auroral vision of the Caucasus – he disappeared.

His *murids* and I searched for him for weeks, asked everybody who knew him for any information they might have. The only fact we gleaned came from his employer, the grocer, who related that Cloud-Dervish had suddenly announced that he had glimpsed a new path.

I felt desolate.

Yet…

Although, as Cloud-Dervish had predicted, I never achieved the purity that would have given me a glimpse of The Godhead, I did experience occasionally, in sudden ecstatic states, nano-perceptions of the natures of the visible and the invisible.

And I learned some recondite truths.

About clouds, for instance: how they use the alphabets of sky, sea, land and fire, to narrate all that has happened and all that is happening and all that will happen; how one can read these narratives everywhere – even as imprints on rooftops – and osmose into the spirits of not only Mesopotamian, Hittite, Greek, Persian, Ottoman, Jewish, Muslim and Christian peoples, but also into those of Africa, Europe, India, China, Australia, Oceania and the Americas; how, most importantly, we attain the gnosis that the divisions fomented by our religions, races, flags, cultures and wealth offend The Divine Presence's infinitely creative multiplicity, that no matter who we are, we are citizens of the world, born under the same clouds and that, therefore, we have the obligation to sanctify life – all life.

But – perhaps most importantly – because Cloud-Dervish always exposed the wounds in his soul readily, I learned what an unremitting affliction displacement is and how, lacking consummate remedies, it can never be healed.

Destiny – sceptics would say Chance – led me to Cloud-Dervish some ten years later.

By then I was living in England, a self-displaced person still searching for God, this time, paradoxically, as a budding historian ensconced in the British Library researching Moorish Andalusia where Jewish-Sufi brotherhoods had blossomed.

I caught sight of him – of all things – in a BBC newsreel.

He was not in İstanbul but in Sicily. And not as a *Murshid* but as an aid worker with the UN Refugee Agency in the Pozzallo Reception Centre. He was helping with the identification of a boatload of African and Middle Eastern migrants who, but for the interception of the Italian Coast Guard, would have perished – like many of their fellow migrants – in the Mediterranean.

I rushed to Pozzallo immediately and contacted him.

On his suggestion, we met at the Cabrera Tower. (For some reason that I never had the wits to explore, he loved strongholds.) I assume the Cabrera Tower reminded him – it certainly reminded me – of our meetings and rituals at the Rumeli Fortress.

We embraced. (We had never embraced during my time as his *murid*.)

He had aged considerably and looked frail, but the lambency of his turquoise eyes had not dimmed.

I asked where he had been all these years and what he had been doing.

He smiled and gazed at the sea stretching before us. 'I've been with refugees. All over Europe. These days they need to know about The Divine Presence more than anybody else.'

I stared at him, trying to see in the depths of his eyes the revelation behind his decision.

He smiled. 'I won't ask where you've been. The crow's-feet on your face tell me you're still nowhere.'

'Yes – still nowhere.'

He closed his eyes.

Not wanting to impinge on whatever issues he was wrestling with, I watched and waited.

Eventually, his eyes still closed, he spoke. 'I lost my path, my brother. Rather I diverted to another path. I'm still a Sufi enamoured of The Godhead. But I'm also unfaithful to Him. I've fallen in love with the Suffering Earth. I've embraced the destitute – *the other* – the stranger you Jews are commanded to love. There are billions of them. Can one conjoin with both the sacred and the ill-starred?'

'Surely your new path can only be one of the innumerable ones that lead to The Divine Presence.'

'Maybe. I keep hoping that. But doubts remain.'

'Doubts are better than complacency.'

'I'll tell you what I've come to know. I think that's why God arranged for us to meet. He knows why I've fallen in love with the earth. He knows I'll only confide in you.'

'I'm listening.'

'What displacement means is obvious to you and me – but not to much of the world. So spread the word wherever you can.'

'My voice is not as strong as yours.'

'Sometimes one voice – no matter how faint – is enough. So listen. We might never meet again.'

'Don't say that.'

'Listen. Just listen!'

Here, as best as I can relate, is what he said.

But is what he said obvious to us all?

'The vessels that harbour morality – what happens when Evil breaks them? You Jews are commanded to repair them. But consider this: in every spillage something vital trickles away. In the case of the vessels that trickle is the life-force.

'People don't recognise it as such. They ignore it as effluence. If it trickles towards those fortunate enough to be well rooted in safe soils, it is calumniated as "invasion". Compassion is expediently purged. Eyes that see the seepage as waste that must be restored and regenerated are forcibly blindfolded.

'Yet this trickle of life-force is, by its very nature, deathless. And the commandment given to it by none other than The Godhead is to extend deathlessness, to breed history.

'At the tragic end of the "invasion" we find millions of refugees – worthy souls who have managed to flee persecution in their homeland for dissension, opposition to regimes, internecine wars, ethnic cleansing and, not least, for fidelity to a faith that fanatics of ruling faiths regard as false.

'Still at the tragic end there are the so-called economic migrants – the downtrodden who, facing marginalisation – not least, starvation – in impoverished countries, bravely undertake the illegal, perilous and sometimes fatal odysseys in the hope of finding jobs that, in all likelihood, will rob them of their dignity and identity.

'At the clement end of the "invasion" there are the émigrés who have expatriated themselves for personal reasons. They are often career chasers or artists of various disciplines or simply people who want better or different lives. Often acceptable to the host country, they appear to be comfortable with their expatriation.

'That's when we falsify the tragedy. We resist admitting that we are all exiles. We deny that the exilic state carries a deep sense of divestiture; that for most exiles this sense creates an unconscious anguish which mourns the loss of a heritage that should never have been lost – namely, roots.

'But it is in roots that salvation lies. Roots can – and do – transplant themselves wherever providence takes them – even in hostile soils. Roots are Nature's mothers. They spin out life forever by giving birth, if need be, in sandy or icy or rocky holes in the wilderness.

'True, the replanted roots will never be as they were in their original habitat. But they will ensure deathlessness. And they will evolve until they emerge as a new species that contains both their original traits and the traits obtained by their evolution.

'Yes, occasionally there will be the odd root that will prove poisonous – like today's extremist Islam. But, whatever the poison, the life-force – once a trickle – will always find its antidote because it is deathless. Thus life will continue.

'Thus the history of migration will chronicle the history of humanity.

'Consequently, should I ever ascend to The Divine Presence, I will praise Him for devising displacement as a *natural* predisposition and shout the Ultimate Truth: THANK YOU, BELOVED, FOR MAKING LIFE DEATHLESS!'

Cloud-Dervish died the next day.

According to the UN Refugee Agency he was seen whirling on the beach early in the morning and suffered a massive heart attack.

I refuse to believe that.

He died either because he attained union with The Godhead or – forgive me for being Jewish here – renounced his life as a *kapparah* – an offering – so that his beloved migrants could root themselves somewhere and live on in deathlessness.

A. L. Kennedy
INAPPROPRIATE STARING

'Look at that one.'

'Where?'

'The little one. There. He's a cheeky one, isn't he?'

'Where?'

'There. Right there. You don't know how to spot them, you don't.'

'Oh, yeah... Fast, isn't he?'

'And cheeky.'

'He's into everything. Look at that.'

'I was looking. You were the one that didn't notice him.'

'Is it a him?'

'Of course. A girl wouldn't be like that. Girls aren't into everything. Girls are quiet. Should be.'

'You can't tell, though, can you? Not with that lot. I mean, they're all like that. See? Running about and climbing and getting in everywhere... Whole swarm of them.'

'They can't be a swarm – that's bees.'

'He'd be in your windows and up on the roof and sitting on your chairs all at once... That's a fact. I've read they're very strong. Impulsive – that's the word.'

'He's a boy. Boys are like that. Look at his little face. That's a boy, that is. And there's his little fingers.'

'There's his dirty little fingers.'

'Well, he's been playing, hasn't he? Oh, and here's Mum... And she's not happy with him, you can tell. I can tell... A mother knows a mother, no matter what. You can be different as anything, but a mother knows when she sees a mother. And he's caught on that she's cross – he's nervous. Wants to hold her hand. You always wanted to hold my hand when I was going to give you a row, remember? She'll clout him, I bet.'

'Well, she can't give him a row, can she. They don't exactly speak.'

'They understand each other.'

'I doubt it... Ah – you didn't expect that. Wrong there, weren't you?'

'Giving him cuddles instead. Well, that's sweet. He's got round her. That's how you used to get round me – give me the big brown eyes and put up your arms for a hug.'

'Dunno what you mean.'

'You still do that with me. Early training, that is. And you get spoiled. Do you carry on that way with Pauline?'

'Why would Pauline want to give me a row?'

'I should imagine she'd have lots of reasons. Why isn't she here, anyway?'

'Work.'

'Didn't want to be with the mother-in-law.'

'She's working, I said. They must be strong... Her lifting him like that. I mean he's got to be a bit of a weight.'

'She'll be used to it. And they are strong, aren't they? I mean, they're stronger than us.'

'Stronger than you.'

'Cheeky boy.'

'Sitting about and staring at the telly, eating chocolate brazils and mini pizzas... Pauline does spinning and free weights and all that – cardio vascular.'

'Personal trainer now, are you? And I don't want to look like a weightlifter. She'll end up built like a bloke. She's got mannish shoulders.'

'She's got stamina.'

'Don't be disgusting to your mother. And what would you want me to have stamina for – cleaning the kitchen?'

'When do you clean that kitchen?'

'Cheeky boy... I spoiled you.'

'Yeah, I'm horrible... I'm a terrible son. Hey, do you think that one's ill? Him under the blanket. I wonder where they get the blankets...'

'What, him? Leastways, I think it's a him. Can't get much of an idea about him, can we... No, he's sleeping. I think. And I suppose they feel the cold the way we do. Or a bit, anyway.'

'Could be hiding – I've seen 'em do that. Maybe he's hiding.'

'We can see him.'

'It's not us he's hiding from, is it?'

'I've read they creep about. Or someone told me.'

'We don't know how they work, do we, I mean it stands to reason they've got ways of knowing each other and they'll have fights with some and like others and there's mums and kids...'

'I think people send in blankets and stuff for them to have and do what they want with. I think.'

'And they'll fancy each other...'

'Don't talk about it like that.'

'Like what? It's just nature. It's just mating. It's animals making other little animals.'

'I've told you, don't be disgusting... His mum's fond of him. She's carried him all along and up there.'

'So she's a mum – she's his mum. That's all instincts, isn't it – with them. It's the same with anything. When I was six or seven, you remember that cat had kittens and I picked one of them up – just a kid and I didn't know better – and the mother clawed all across the back of my hand.'

'And she was a good cat the rest of the time.'

'Not that day.'

'Well, she seems fond of him, doesn't she? His mum. We're not the same – but you can tell. That's all I'm saying.'

'Want her round your house, would you? Give her tea. Have her kiddie shitting on your floor.'

'Babies mess themselves... Oh, my goodness – he's big. He's a big one.'

'Where'd he come from?'

'He's got a turn of speed.'

'You wouldn't want him heading for you. He'd tear you in half.'

'The size of him... You see pictures in magazines and places, but you don't understand until you see them for yourself.'

'You'd have a heart attack before he even got to you. Just thinking about it... I bet he'd break your neck with one hand, I bet you he could.'

'He looked at me.'

'No, not at you. Don't be daft.'

'Yes he did.'

'He's just looking at everything, it's not ***at you***. It's just... you're one of the things in the way of him searching about. He doesn't understand.'

'He looked at me.'

'You're all right – he can't get to you. He can't get near you.'

'Sometimes they get out.'

'There's electric fences and all sorts of stuff. We're safe here.'

'I don't think so. I don't like how he looked at me. That was personal.'

'It can't be – he's not a person – he can't look like a person looks at you. It's not like you stared into his big brown eyes and you could tell he was thinking. He's not thinking – they don't.'

'Will you listen – he's not thinking the way you think, but he's thinking. I can tell.'

'You're scaring yourself. It's not like he's going to leap out and grab you, is it?'

'Don't say that. Don't. I shall have nightmares.'

'Well, that's your choice.'

'You wouldn't like it if he got out and came for you. You wouldn't like to see that coming across a room at you, would you? See – I'll make you scared. Pauline would say running away from him was cardio vascular, would she? She'd like it, then, would she?'

'Well, of course she wouldn't. And I wouldn't. Who would? It's not going to happen, though, is it? That was a joke. I was joking.'

'They can hear us.'

'But they don't know what we're saying. Anyway, it was on the radio – you have to make yourself look as big as possible and talk as loud as you can and that keeps them back. It doesn't matter that they don't understand. You have authority and they fear authority.'

'No, you do that with bears. I read that, too – it was for bears.'

'It would work on him.'

'I don't think so... He doesn't seem to like his missus much. Or the kiddie.'

'You don't know those two are anything to do with him. Might be someone else's. Might be anyone's, I expect. I don't suppose she's sure...'

'Shush, I don't want to think about that... Ah, here we go – food. That's got them running.'

'Yeah, we came for a bit of a show and some action. And they're hungry, aren't they? It's like they're starving. All that grabbing.'

'The big chap's got his. In and away.'

'Instinct – they're all about instinct.'

'No, no, there – he's gone over and handed some of it to the missus and the little one. They're getting some.'

'Sharing's instinct as well. It's all instinct. You take care of your own. We take care of our own – they take care of their own.'

'You don't take care of me.'

'I'm here, aren't I? We take care. We have civilisation and toilets. We have families, proper families... Those ones are fighting.'

'That's not fighting – not the way they could fight.'

'Yeah, more of a scuffle. They're vicious, of course, if they get going. Really nasty. And they've all got a temper.'

'He's good with the kiddie, though... They both are. Breaking off bits so he can have them. Sweet. You've got to say they can be sweet.'

'Everything's sweet sometimes. Snakes probably are sweet sometimes. You're either scared to death or you want to hug everything – that's how you are...'

'Snakes aren't sweet.'

'Yeah, they can be.'

'Of course they're not.'

'To other snakes. How'd you think you get more snakes? Big snakes make baby snakes.'

'She's got you obsessed, that Pauline – all stamina and sex. You didn't used to be like that. Talking about animals and instincts the whole time.'

'You should think what you're saying sometimes, you should.'

'Or you could take your own advice.'

'What's that supposed to mean?'

'The dad's picked him up – see? You can't say that's not sweet.'

'I didn't say.'

'And he's having tickles. I wouldn't have believed that if you'd told me – a brute like him and he's swinging the kid about and having tickles.'

'Don't say it.'

'Just like us.'

'Yeah, except for all the ways they're completely different. Invite them round for dinner, would you? He'll make that kid sick – it's just eaten. You shouldn't swing an infant when it's just eaten.'

'How would you know? Pauline won't give you any kids, you know – she's too fond of her figure... I could have kept my figure and then there'd be no you... Selfish... She's selfish. And I'd rather have any of them in my house than your mate Paul. They'd smell better.'

'Ha, that's not wrong. But Paul likes you. Since his mum died, he likes you.'

'But it's peculiar. I don't need him coming round – he says he's mending things, but he's not.'

'The old boy under the blanket's awake, then. That's some face he's got on him – been in the wars.'

'I think they heal fast, though. I mean, we wouldn't survive it and they just keep on. You can knock them about and they barely notice.'

'They're part of nature, like I was saying, that's the thing. You don't need stitches and antibiotics and that if you're nature.'

'He's limping.'

'Taking his blanket with him. The others might get it off him otherwise.'

'Poor old sod – he's after a bit of the food and there's none left.'

'You snooze, you lose.'

'I didn't teach you to be like that.'

'Everyone taught me that. It's a competitive world. That's nature, too.'

'They seem sad.'

'What?'

'All of them. When they just sit and stare out – their eyes. They seem sad.'

'You're reading things in again – they're not sad.'

'They seem sad.'

'It's just the way their faces are. They all look like that all the time.'

'No, they seem sad. When they don't look angry, they look sad.'

'Well, that's all they've got, isn't it? They get angry and they look angry and then they go back to looking like themselves. They're not sad. What are you going to do – send them a blanket?'

'I'd send a blanket to the kiddie. Can we do that?'

'Soft touch, you are. Have you seen enough, because I'm hungry. Will we go and have lunch?'

'If you want. They still look sad, though.'

'I've explained it to you – their faces are made that way – they're not sad.'

Hassan Abdulrazzak

THE DOG-SHAPED HOLE IN THE GARDEN

I'll get to my refugee story in a minute but first let's jump to the happy ending. Well, a sort of happy ending.

The setting is my parents' house in New Malden, Surrey. I was thirteen and incredibly happy to be once again living in a house with a big garden after many years of country hopping and staying in cramped accommodation. And what's more, I was super excited about the prospect of getting a dog. My younger sister, who was just as excited, was a junior member of the Royal Society for the Prevention of Cruelty to Animals (RSPCA) and she had suggested we get a dog through them. All we had to do was pass a routine check. When the day of the inspection arrived, I was the only one present at home to meet the lady from the RSPCA. She rang the bell and my chubby self opened the door for her and I instantly switched to ultra-polite mode, which I always did upon meeting English people. As an Iraqi kid recently arrived in Britain, I was desperate for them to have a good impression of me and my family.

The RSPCA lady had a slim figure and shoulder length black hair. She may have worn glasses or I might have put them on her face in later years as I recalled this episode.

What I am sure about is that she carried a clipboard. I don't recall her name but let's call her Ann. She looked like an Ann, prim and serious (apologies to all the Anns reading this for the crude generalisation). I showed her around the house as she checked the various rooms and ticked little boxes on her form. As Ann explained about the various dogs they have and which breeds she would recommend, I nodded and smiled and answered her questions with chubby politeness. Everything was going swimmingly. I believe she had ticked all the boxes on her form by the time we had walked across the patio and reached the annexe room that leads to the back of our garage, a room disconnected from the rest of the house containing the boiler. I should have kept my mouth shut as the tour came to an end then escorted Ann to the front door and bid her goodbye. But instead I asked, to her instant horror, whether we could keep the dog in the boiler room.

To my mind this was a perfectly reasonable proposition. My knowledge about keeping dogs came primarily from Disney cartoons that I had watched in Baghdad, Cairo and Algiers. Didn't Americans, who are sort of cousins of the English, keep dogs in smallish, brown, hut-like kennels in their gardens? Didn't Mickey Mouse keep Pluto in such a place? To my thirteen-year-old mind, the boiler room, being spacious and very warm, seemed so much better than a kennel in the garden. But the horrified look on Ann's face told me that I had put my foot in it.

'A dog needs love, a dog must be treated like a member of the family, he has to live with you. How could you think that keeping it locked up in the boiler room is any way to treat a dog?'

'Well, we don't have to lock the room, we could leave the door open.'

Once again this seemed like sound reasoning, judging by cartoon kennels whose doors were non-existent, but it only made Ann more furious to think that I was seriously contemplating the idea. I tried to back-pedal by saying, 'Look, it will be fine for the dog to live inside the house with us,' and here I really should have deployed a full stop and ended the sentence. It could have saved the day.

'But the thing is, my mum is worried about it leaving hair all over the new furniture so I just thought this might be a good solution.'

That was it for Ann. She scribbled furiously in her sheet, so furiously I thought the pen was going to pierce the plastic clipboard like a knife.

'I'm recommending that you be denied the right to have a dog. Furthermore, I will make sure that your house remains on our blacklist for as long as possible.' My memory from that point on is hazy so it might be an exaggeration to say 'and with that she stormed out', but then again, it might not.

I realised that day that it was going to be a long, hard struggle to learn all the rules of my new homeland.

My dream of owning a dog started back in Baghdad in the late 1970s. My parents and I lived in my grandfather's house. Three storeys high with a 180 degree garden, it was the perfect playground for a young child. The sky was almost always blue and the roses fragrant like no other roses that I have encountered since. My father grew up with a smart dog that he loved called Cyro. Alas, the dog was poisoned but stories of his escapades made me want to own a dog and Dad was contemplating buying one for me.

In the Iraq of the late 1970s, life was extremely good for middle-class families like my own. Dad worked as a sociologist in a research centre and Mum as a paediatrician. The oil boom meant that salaries were high and the dinar was worth around two British pounds. My aunties would spend the summer visiting London to buy the latest fashions, which they found highly affordable. My parents used any excuse to throw lavish parties. The adults would celebrate my birthday by getting gloriously drunk and dancing till the small hours to the latest Boney M records. In the summertime we would sleep on the flat rooftop under a canopy of dazzlingly bright stars and I would pester Dad to name the various constellations.

A change took place that didn't seem so significant at first. The old president stepped down and a man I had never heard of called Saddam Hussein took his place. At school they made us sing songs dedicated to him. At home, my parents were cautious to speak of him though at the time I was not aware of it. Later I learned that people were arrested and disappeared because children had let slip their parents' low opinion of the new president at school. Soon after he assumed power, Saddam began to crack down on members of the Iraqi Communist Party (ICP) who were the main opposition to his Ba'ath Party. I didn't know this at the time, but my family were associated with the ICP. Family members who were active in the party began to flee. When I would ask why this uncle was heading to Moscow or that auntie was heading to Prague, I would only get vague answers. Then one day, men with serious moustaches came knocking on our door. Would my father care to join them for a little chat? Mum's face grew ashen as the hours passed slowly and Dad hadn't returned. I knew something was wrong, but no one, not my mother, nor my grandmother, would tell me why Dad was suddenly taken away.

When he returned, Dad wouldn't tell me who those men were or what they wanted and life seemed to go back to normal. As summer approached we went to the open-air cinema where I saw *Lady and the Tramp* and became lost in dreams of owning a spaghetti-eating dog. When I broached the subject with Dad, he seemed less enthusiastic about it than before. He was holding something back.

First grade was over and I was looking forward to what I thought would be another lazy, hot Baghdad summer where

I would run around the house in my underwear, wielding the wooden sword that our local carpenter had made for me and scratch the inside of our horizontal freezer to scoop handfuls of ice with which to cool myself. And who knows maybe this would be the year when we would finally get a dog.

Then out of the blue my parents announced we were going abroad. Wait a minute, why is Dad selling his beloved red Mercedes? Does it cost that much to go on holiday? We took a cab to the airport and all the adults, Mum, Dad and Grandma, were visibly tense. I thought going on holiday was supposed to be fun. Their tension increased with every step: as we entered the airport; as we had our passports checked; as we got on the airplane. Finally when we took off, I heard them breathe a collective sigh of relief. My father kept pestering the stewardess for more and more whisky.

It was only when we arrived in Cairo and settled in my uncle's flat that I began to understand what had happened. The men with the serious moustaches who came to our house were Ba'ath Party members. They wanted my dad to join their party or else. Dad knew that those who did not comply with their demands could end up at the dreaded Palace of the End where they would be summarily executed. This was the fate of many Communists and, though Dad was not a member of the ICP, our family's affiliation with the party was enough to arouse the suspicions of the government. Dad had read enough about the rise of the Nazis to realise that a similar thing was happening in Iraq under Saddam. If he had capitulated and joined the Ba'athists, he would soon have to write reports on his friends and colleagues. It was a case of damned if you do and damned if you don't. So the only way out was to leave the country. Money had to be raised quickly through the sale of the car. The tension at the airport was due to my family not being sure whether we would be on a list of those barred from leaving.

At first, I wasn't aware that we had become refugees. Our stay with my uncle felt like an extended holiday but Dad could not be a burden on his brother for long and there were no jobs to be had in Egypt. He was offered a university teaching position in Algeria and so, once again, we packed our bags and moved countries. Friends of my parents offered us their flat to stay in upon arrival. It was then that I began to feel the weight of what we had lost. I remember the gloom that engulfed my family on our first night in Algiers. None of us could sleep properly, each lost in thoughts of what we had left behind: the house, the car, the family outings, the parties, the garden, the fragrant roses, the canopy of stars. Maybe Saddam would die of a heart attack, I thought, and we could go back. How wrong I was.

The Algerian kids in the neighbourhood were alien to me as they spoke a mixture of French, Berber and twisted Arabic. I communicated with them in classical Arabic, which is the language taught at school that no one actually speaks. The scene was absurd, like coming across a group of children in Britain who can only play with each other by conversing in Shakespearean English. Later we moved to our own flat in a building that possessed all the charm of a Communist era Soviet block. The roads outside were never finished because every time the council tried to lay down gravel for tarring the road, the kids would steal the stones for fun. So wading in mud on the way to school became the norm. Worst of all, there was a scarcity of books in the country. In Baghdad, I had grown up with an abundance of books: illustrated Western classics, colourful comics and the works of Naguib Mahfouz. At night, I would dream of going back to our house in Baghdad and raiding the bookshelves for things to read, only to wake up realising that I was still in Algiers.

It was my Cairo uncle who finally decided that for the sake of my education and that of my sister, it would be best if we moved to Britain where he had studied in the 1950s.

He bought the house in New Malden and I was filled with joy to have a garden again. True, I did not speak English, but I quickly noticed that the bookshops in Britain were filled to the brim and if only I could crack the language, all that knowledge would be mine. My diary entries slowly began to change from Arabic to English. As I adjusted to my new life, I realised that my idyllic Baghdad existence was never coming back. We had fallen out of Eden and it would be best to get used to life on earth.

* * *

In 2013, a lifetime later, I returned to Iraq, but this time to Erbil, one of the safe cities in the north, rather than to Baghdad, which was still dangerous and chaotic a decade after the US-led invasion. As I had never been to Erbil before, the trip did not feel like a homecoming.

I was interested, as a playwright, in finding out more about the Kurdish Syrian refugees who had fled to northern Iraq in the wake of the civil war that had broken out in their country. The first refugee camp I visited was Domiz, which is three hours' drive from Erbil. The Iraqi Kurdish driver who took me to the camp complained about how the Syrian refugees were ruining his son's building trade because they were willing to work for less than the going rate. I was sympathetic towards the plight of his son, but at the same time I knew from experience that no one chooses to become a refugee.

In Domiz, the scale of the Syrian disaster became apparent to me for the camp was the size of a town with tents stretching into the distance as far as the eye could see. They had fled horrors that I could only imagine. The first wave of refugees had escaped the shelling of their homes by Bashar al-Assad's government forces. The more recent arrivals had survived the onslaught of Islamists who were murdering the Kurds because they were not Muslim enough in their eyes.

Another camp I visited a day later, called Kawergosk, was newly established and hence much less organised than Domiz. Many of the families there were sleeping out in the open under the 40 degree sun, desert dust swirling all around them. Some mistook me for a journalist and pleaded with me to tell the world about the long journey on foot that they had undertaken to get to the camp, the people they saw collapsing along the way, their sick children, their desperation for a tent to shield them from the relentless sun. I felt powerless as I listened to these tales of woe. Everything that my family and I went through paled into insignificance by comparison. We were sheltered by money, my parents' education and our connections abroad. It struck me that had any of these factors not been in place, had we stayed in Iraq till the first Gulf War, had we experienced the Western-imposed sanctions on the country and the catastrophic collapse in the value of the dinar, we too could have ended up in refugee camps as so many Iraqi families did, experiencing the same dire conditions that I was seeing all around me in Kawergosk.

One of the many sad stories I came across was that of two siblings, the first in their family to reach university. Lorraine dreamt of becoming a lawyer while her brother Rawan wanted to work in the oil sector. As refugees, these dreams of pursuing higher education were dashed because there were not enough places in the Iraqi Kurdish universities to accommodate all the refugee students. Lorraine was determined not to become a victim by busying herself with organising camp life to make it more bearable. She was the inspiration for Ghalia, the heroine of my play, *Dhow Under the Sun*, which was performed in the United Arab Emirates.

Having visited Syria before the war, I knew what the refugees I met were missing, particularly those who had lived in the capital Damascus with its ancient alleyways, picturesque cafés, impressive mosques and exquisite old houses, adorned with water fountains and hidden gardens. They too had fallen out of Eden. They too were having to live on earth. However, their earth was a much more inhospitable place than anything I had experienced.

Back in Britain, I felt a renewed sense of gratitude for my life but also a greater anger towards politicians and some strands of the media who play the fear card and press the buttons of the population to make them suspicious of all the refugees arriving on Europe's shores. The neighbouring countries to Syria that have taken in the refugees are under tremendous strain to cope. Their economies and infrastructure are nowhere near as developed as ours. We cannot walk away from this catastrophe.

Our house in Baghdad is no longer there. It has been demolished and the garden dug up. In my first play, ***Baghdad Wedding***, I recreated the house with words, complete with rooftop access to the stars. If I ever get the chance to return to Baghdad, it will be to a city that I won't recognise. The Baghdad that my family and I knew lives now only in dreams, stories and the memories we share. The same will be true for many of those who have fled Syria.

Whenever I visit my parents' house in New Malden, I feel grateful for the safety, opportunity and welcome that Britain offered us. The only thing still missing from the house is a dog. Perhaps the RSPCA ban has been lifted. Or maybe I have grown used to the dog-shaped hole in the garden.

Sue Gee

GLIMPSE

A man is sitting in Gavin's garden, on a hard wooden chair. There's another one next to it, standing on the uncut grass. The garden is autumnal and untidy; likewise the house. Likewise Gavin, alone again, shambling about the kitchen in his holey old sweater, looking for a clean mug. Two clean mugs. A brimming ashtray sits on the table next to a heap of newspapers, junk mail and general muddle. Rinsing the mugs, both deeply tea-stained, he hears Celia's sigh.

'Why can't you *clear up*? Look at it all.'

His letter to her, unposted, lies on the table, a sad thing. It's taken him days to write.

'Oh, Gavin.'

There'd been so many things for her to sigh about: the smoking; the mess and the muddle; his failure to notice. And not enough money, staying up late trying to make more, while she lay reading in bed, and waiting. Not enough of that, either, by the end.

'Good book?'

'Oh, Gavin.'

Yet at the beginning—

As the kettle comes to the boil he has – yet again – a brief, piercing vision: Celia, naked and adoring, and – once again – he is sick with longing. How could someone like her have wanted someone like him? She must have thought she was getting an artist, a bit of bohemia, finding instead just this hopeless bloke.

He drops a teabag into each mug, and glances out through the unwashed window. The man on the chair is sitting stiffly, his right leg stretched out, hardly looking about him, as though to look about him would be impolite. The late afternoon sunshine falls on bindweed, a straggle of misty blue Michaelmas daisies, the last old roses clambering over the fence. And though the muddy grass is waiting for its last cut, and though it's probably getting a bit cold, it's nice out there: nicer than in here, where Gavin hasn't had a guest for quite a while. Celia was the last person to behold the overflowing bin, the boxes of stuff in the hall, the ashtrays. They were everywhere.

'You've *got* to give up.'

He'd tried, and he couldn't. He tried to clear up, and the mess came back. She'd tried to change him, and failed.

'What's the *matter* with you?'

He knew he was vague, thoughtless, just trying to get through. A come-and-go freelance life, a son far away, a long-distant marriage. A couple of women since, but no one who'd meant as much as she did.

'Please don't go.'

Work had dried up, and the house had felt horrible when she was at work herself, swishing down the stairs in her boots and long coat. How could he ever have thought she would stay? He made a huge effort, emptying things, throwing things out, cleaning the bath.

'Is that a bit better?'

'Do you want me to give you a medal?'

That had hurt. And then what had been good between them – the sudden excitement of two such different people – passed, irrecoverably. But still—

'Please don't go. What will I do, without you?'

Workless days stretched ahead. The prospect of trying,

again, to kick-start a flailing career – the emails, the phone calls, the *just wondering if there's anything, I'm free for the next week or two* – all felt impossible.

'What will I do?'

'I don't know, Gavin. Why don't you volunteer, or something? Think about someone else, for once.'

Out in the garden, the light is deepening. It's cool, and Ola shifts on the chair, and moves his right leg, so painful still. He's not been invited inside, and he hadn't expected to be, not really: he's grown used to being outside, to spending days limping along the streets, though finally he no longer sleeps there. He's slept in doorways, on benches, on night buses, at the back of a betting shop, the back of a library, until someone's kicked him out. Finally, he has a room in a hostel, but it closes its doors after breakfast. He'll be back there at six this evening, crossing the huge high hall with its smell of disinfectant, to queue with all the others in a cavernous dining room. Finally, he has two meals a day. He'll slowly climb the bare stairs to the showers, the dormitories, his leg giving pain with every step. Two dozen others sleep in his dorm: he doesn't care. At last he has a bed.

He has a caseworker, too. An energetic young woman in the place he found through the hostel, scanning the notice board with all the others, skimming over drug abuse, domestic violence, police, yoga.

Are you seeking asylum?

Now, he has somewhere to go on Wednesdays, and someone who listens, and does not look shocked, though Ola himself was shocked to hear his own sobbing, loud and uncontrollable, when he finally told his story. Now, in a different place, he has a doctor, who has seen his naked body, the twisted leg and the scars, and mapped them onto the outline of a human male. That made him sob, too: remembering. Knowing that he had been believed. He will have a lawyer, though it will take a while. And he has a house, an English house, to visit, where an Englishman wants to meet him.

Traffic roars by on the main road, a couple of blocks from here. A few quiet streets away, they are observing the Sabbath. Gavin puts the two mugs on a tray, takes them off again, and wipes it. He puts a milk bottle on it, then takes it off, and pours the milk into a jug. Likewise the bag of sugar: into a bowl. He finds two teaspoons, rinses them, opens the packet of biscuits he bought this morning and sets them out on a plate. Okay. No – wait a minute. He picks up his cigarettes, lights up. God, that's better.

Then he opens the back door, onto the strip of concrete that runs alongside the house, and goes out into the strip of garden. Where he stops, seeing Olly – yes? – sitting up stiffly no longer, but bent double, his head in his hands.

Traffic roars by, and a bus changes gear, and speeds up. And although he has seen and heard countless buses since his arrival in the city, now, in a garden – and he has not been in a garden once, since his arrival – Ola is suddenly taken to quite another place. He sees the compound of his childhood, the huts, the bony wandering goats, and himself on a mat made of banana leaves, sitting with the other children in the skimpy shade of a marula tree. An old blackboard is propped on an easel, a worn creased map pinned to the frame. The teacher is pointing with a stick that is sometimes – not often – used to beat them, when they are bad, and they are all chanting together, sitting cross-legged on their woven mats.

'Paris is the capital of France! London is the capital of England!'

The sun beats down on the hard baked earth; in the distance, he can hear the National Bus rumble by on the unmade road that leads – where? To Paris? He is seven years old, and has no idea. He knows he is very hungry.

But then, as the Saturday traffic here grows louder, Ola sees his own city, the crumbling, impoverished city of his adult life, where he trained, and taught, and married, and had his children, and struggled to feed and clothe them, as everyone was struggling. Soldiers were everywhere: in doorways, on rooftops, bumping down the dusty streets in open trucks, suddenly stopping, leaping out, racing through the crowded market.

'Hey! You!'

Or sometimes they came after dark.

He joined the secret group in opposition, attended secret meetings. And now, unstoppably, beginning to shake, he flashes to the night of his capture, the drive through the unlit city streets, the peeling shuttered building where he was held in darkness. What happened then – to him, to the screaming others in other cells – is what made him sob so wildly, so horribly, when he finally recounted it. He remembers it now, sweating all over, and the night of his escape.

He sees his wife, Dayo (Joy arrives), held in a last embrace, and his children sleeping in a moonlit row, not stirring as he whispers goodbye. Baako (First-born), Emeka (God did great deeds), Chiemeka (God has done very well), Mudiwa (Beloved). And he knows that the last, the little one he has never seen, who kicks in Dayo's belly as he holds her close and weeping, will be named Abidemi (Born while father is away).

He had felt good when he rang the doorbell here: nervous, but hopeful. Now, as it all comes flashing back – unspooling uncontrollably, triggered just by a bus on a busy road, as anything can trigger it all, at any time – he doubles up, puts his head in his hands.

Gavin tentatively clears his throat, carefully sets down the tray on the other hard kitchen chair, inhales and lets out a stream of smoke.

'Olly?'

Ola's shoulders are shaking. He looks up, his face streaming with tears. Gavin looks quickly away.

'Sorry. So sorry.' Ola moves his aching leg a little, winces, wipes his cheek. 'So sorry,' he says again.

'Please.' Gavin stands there, not knowing what to do. 'Would you like me to leave you—'

Ola shakes his head, fumbling in his pocket. He pulls out a handkerchief, wipes his face, breathes in hard. 'Sometimes—' He hesitates. 'Sometimes the past—'

'Sure,' says Gavin. It's a word he uses too often, another thing that got on Celia's nerves, and it sounds meaningless now, but he knows all about the way the past floods in. Or does he? Standing in his unkempt autumn garden, where he has sometimes himself sat assailed by everything that lies so uselessly behind him, he has a glimpse of what those words might mean now. Another, terrible country. Another life entirely.

'Sure,' he says again, and gestures to the tea tray. 'Help yourself.'

Ola takes a mug, and slowly pours in milk and stirs in sugar, and Gavin sets the tray on the muddy grass and sits down beside him. He raises his own mug.

'Cheers,' he says, idiotically, and wants to kick himself. But: 'Cheers, Olly.'

'Ola,' says Ola, taking a first sip. 'Olamilekan. It means—' He drinks again, gives a wry smile. 'It means: My wealth is increasing.'

'Well,' says Gavin drily, after a moment, and returns the smile. 'That's good.'

Ola nods, and lifts his mug towards him. 'Cheers.' The hot sweet tea feels exactly what he needed.

'Biscuit?'

'Thank you.'

'Cigarette?'

Ola shakes his head. Gavin takes another long deep drag. Neither knows what to say next. The traffic on the main road thunders by. And they sit there in a silence that, surprisingly to each of them, does not feel difficult or uneasy, but more – the word comes to Gavin like a benediction – more like quietude, as the smoky air grows cooler and the last of the sun lights the last of the clambering roses.

Joan Smith
TO AVOID WORSE

The best-known images of Anne Frank show a teenager with dark hair and a lively expression. Her diaries, written while she was in hiding for two years with her family in a secret apartment in Amsterdam, are powerful evidence of the resilience of the human spirit. Despite the onerous restrictions on her family, and the ever-present fear of discovery, Anne was able to record the thoughts, feelings and ambitions of a clever adolescent girl. But they also tend to obscure what is in some respects the most important part of her story: the fact that her death, like that of so many refugees in the twenty-first century, could have been avoided. Anne and her family were what some sections of the British press would now call – with the stigma that heartless phrase invokes – failed asylum seekers. Her coming-of-age story in the secret annexe is better-known than the increasingly desperate efforts by her father, Otto Frank, to find a safe haven for his family: Anne, her elder sister Margot, and his wife Edith.

One of the most shocking things about the fate of the Frank family is that Otto recognised a threat as soon as the Nazis came to power in Germany in 1933. No one at that point could have imagined the horrors of the concentration camps but there were anti-Semitic demonstrations in Otto's home city, Frankfurt. Otto sent his wife and daughters to stay with his mother-in-law in Aachen while he made arrangements to move his business to the Netherlands. The family was established in Amsterdam by the spring of 1934, just before Anne's fifth birthday. They were among 25,000 Jewish refugees from Germany who arrived in the Netherlands between 1933 and 1938, a small-scale migration that nevertheless caused alarm in the Dutch government.

From 1934 onwards a series of laws were passed to discourage immigrants, including restrictions on access to work, culminating in a circular from the Justice Department in May 1938 that no more refugees would be allowed into the Netherlands. That was only a couple of months after the *Anschluss*, Hitler's invasion and annexation of Austria; in November that year, during *Kristallnacht* or the Night of Broken Glass, hundreds of synagogues and 7,500 Jewish-owned shops were ransacked and set on fire in Germany. The Nazis deported 30,000 male Jews to concentration camps, prompting more than 40,000 German Jews to apply for Dutch visas; only 7,000 were admitted. These events prompted Otto's first attempt to get his family out of Europe: he made an application in 1938 to the American consul in Rotterdam for visas that would allow himself, Edith and the children to go to the US, where Edith's brothers already lived, but nothing came of it. By the beginning of 1939, there were 300,000 people on the waiting list for American visas and borders were closing all around. The situation became more urgent in May 1940 when Germany invaded the Netherlands, prompting a slew of anti-Semitic decrees.

It isn't clear why Otto delayed a second and more concerted attempt to get his family out of the Netherlands until 1941. A cache of documents released in New York in 2007 includes three letters in his handwriting, including a direct appeal to his American friend Nathan Straus Jr, whose father owned Macy's department store. Otto didn't have the $5,000 he needed for visas but Straus was willing to help, agreeing to cover the cost and contacting the US

State Department on the family's behalf. Tragically for the Franks, the American government had recently followed the example of some European countries, instructing US consuls to delay visa approvals on grounds of national security. That was bad enough but Otto also faced travel restrictions, as a Jew, that meant he could not make the journey to the US consulate in Rotterdam to plead his case in person. In September 1941, he decided to try a different avenue, applying for Cuban visas in the hope that from there he could make a personal appeal to get his family into the US. A Cuban visa was granted in December 1941 but cancelled when the US declared war on Germany, ending the family's hopes of escaping from occupied Europe.

On 6 July 1942, they went into hiding in a secret annexe above the offices of one of Otto's old businesses. They survived for just over two years before being betrayed to the Nazis and arrested on 4 August 1944. The Frank family was taken to the Westerbork transit camp, which had originally been set up by the Dutch government to house refugees but was now the starting-point for trains taking prisoners to the concentration camps. On 3 September, the Frank family were placed on the first of the three final transports to Auschwitz-Birkenau, enduring a dreadful three-day journey in cattle trucks to Poland. Otto was immediately separated from the rest of the family, whom he never saw again.

At the end of October, Edith was separated from her daughters, who were sent to the Bergen-Belsen camp in northern Germany. Edith died of starvation at the age of forty-five on 6 January 1945, three weeks before Auschwitz was liberated by Russian soldiers. Anne and Margot died during a typhus epidemic in Bergen-Belsen in February or March 1945, a few weeks before the British army entered the camp. Anne was fifteen at the time of her death, while Margot had probably turned nineteen. At the end of the

Second World War, Otto discovered that he was the only member of the family who had survived.

When he realised that Anne's diaries had not been destroyed, Otto devoted the rest of his life to looking after his younger daughter's literary legacy. He published an edited version of the diaries, omitting comments about his marriage, Anne's strained relations with her mother and her natural curiosity about sex; his impulse to protect the family is understandable, after everything he had endured, but it created an idealised version of Anne. Publication was followed in 1959 by a film, entitled *The Diary of Anne Frank*, which gave the story international recognition while also romanticising it. There are no scenes in the concentration camps, which make an appearance only in one of Anne's nightmares while she is still living in the annexe.

Obviously it is much easier to contemplate Anne alive and well, writing in her diary, than Anne starving in blankets infested with lice in Bergen-Belsen. This is not to question the significance of the diaries or the way in which their survival, against the odds, stands as a rebuke to the right-wing fanatics who created the conditions that killed her. But the portrayal of Anne in popular culture speaks volumes about how we think – how we allow ourselves to think – about refugees. The diaries are a story without an end, broken off when Anne's hiding place was discovered, and that fact is crucial to their enduring appeal. They allow us to think about loss and wasted lives but without dwelling on either the day-to-day horrors of the Holocaust or the missed opportunities that would have brought about her physical – as well as literary – survival. Anne's story has been transformed into a wistful tale about a plucky teenage girl but it is really about what happens when supposedly decent countries erect barriers to terrified refugees, as many of them are doing once again in the twenty-first century.

In 2015, seventy years after Anne's death, another family

was making desperate efforts to escape a brutal dictatorship. By then the Assad dynasty had been in power in Syria for forty-five years, torturing and murdering opponents with a savagery barely acknowledged by the outside world. Hafez al-Assad came to power through the Ba'ath Party, which was founded in Damascus in 1947 by Arab nationalists who admired European fascist regimes, including Nazi Germany; one of the torture devices commonly used in Hafez al-Assad's grim prisons was called the 'German chair'. When Hafez died in 2000, his son Bashar succeeded him, raising brief and illusory hopes in the West that he might make reforms; Tony Blair welcomed Bashar al-Assad to London in December 2002 and even held a joint press conference with him in Downing Street. It was never a realistic proposition and the younger Assad quickly adopted exactly the same methods as his father to retain his family's grip on power.

Inspired by the Arab Spring, an uprising against the regime began in 2011, prompting a protracted civil war and a refugee crisis on a scale that hasn't been witnessed since the Second World War. In the following four years, according to the UNHCR, more than four million people fled Syria and another 7.6 million were internally displaced. Civilians gathered up as much as they could carry and moved from one area of the country to another as fighting raged between the regime, opposition forces and latterly groups of terrorists affiliated to al-Qaeda or the so-called Islamic State. War crimes were committed, including the use by the regime of chemical weapons, while shortages of electricity, water and food made everyday life all but impossible.

In 2012, a Syrian Kurdish barber called Abdullah Shenu decided it was too dangerous to remain in Damascus and moved his family to the northern city of Aleppo. When Aleppo was targeted by heavy shelling, Abdullah, his wife Rihan and their son Galip moved again, this time to the mainly Kurdish town of Kobani on Syria's border with Turkey. But the town failed to provide a safe haven, becoming the site of fierce battles between Kurdish forces and the ruthless fighters of Islamic State.

Abdullah moved to Turkey, a decision that must have been taken with some trepidation, given the unhappy history of that country's Kurdish minority; it was there, it seems, that he became known by the generic surname 'Kurdi', which simply reflects his ethnic origin. After the birth of his younger son, Aylan, Abdullah brought the rest of the family to Istanbul but conditions for Syrian immigrants were harsh. 'Abdullah was the only one working and getting by was difficult and he couldn't stand Istanbul any more,' a friend recalled. In January 2015, Abdullah sent the family back to Kobani but fighting broke out again and a shell destroyed their house. He brought the family back to Istanbul but they had nowhere to live, ending up in a refugee camp. It was at this point, in despair and after three years on the move, that Abdullah seems to have come to the conclusion that he had to get his family out of the area altogether.

Like Otto Frank, Abdullah had family connections in North America, where his sister Teema had lived in Vancouver for two decades. She agreed to act as the family's sponsor – 'it is horrible the way they treat Syrians in Turkey,' she said – and set about raising the funds they needed to support their application for asylum. But the application was turned down, making the family's situation even worse: without official status as refugees they were stranded in Turkey, unable to get exit visas to leave the country. With all legal avenues closed, the couple decided to head for Bodrum, a holiday destination on the Aegean coast popular with British tourists. These days the port is famous for more sinister reasons: it is only fifteen miles by sea from the Greek island of Kos, the nearest entry-point into the European Union, and has become a thriving centre for people-smugglers.

The family stayed in Bodrum for several weeks while Abdullah tried to borrow the money to pay for a clandestine crossing to Kos. His first two attempts failed: one crossing was halted by coastguards who took the refugees back to Turkey, while the smugglers failed to turn up on another occasion. Abdullah decided to try again in the early hours of 2 September, placing his wife, five-year-old Galip and Aylan, who was three by now, in a rubber dinghy. It isn't clear whether he paid people-smugglers or organised the attempt himself, helped by a Turkish captain, but the boat was overcrowded. When sea conditions became rough, the captain panicked and jumped overboard, leaving the frantic refugees struggling to keep it afloat. 'I took over and started steering,' Abdullah said afterwards. 'The waves were so high and the boat flipped. I was holding my wife's hand but my children slipped through my hands. We tried to cling to the boat, but it was deflating. It was dark and everyone was screaming.'

Twelve people died, including Rihan, Galip and Aylan. Like Otto Frank, Abdullah Kurdi found himself the sole survivor of the family he had tried so hard to get to safety. The difference is that a Turkish photographer spotted Aylan's small body, washed up on a beach in Bodrum, and took harrowing pictures that were reproduced around the world: the little boy lies on his front in his red T-shirt and blue shorts, his arms stretched along his sides and his face slightly turned into the sand. A moment later a Turkish policeman, Mehmet Çıplak, lifts him gently from the surf and carries him up the beach. 'When I saw the baby on the beach, I approached and said to myself, "Dear God, I hope he's alive",' Sergeant Çıplak said. 'When I found out he was dead, I was crushed deep down inside. It was a terrible sight, it was a terrible loss.'

Aylan Kurdi did not need to die, any more than Anne Frank. Seventy years apart, their stories are characterised by the same depressingly bureaucratic response to refugees fleeing fascist regimes. The closing of borders to refugees from Nazi Germany is mirrored in the twenty-first century by legal obstacles that force desperate people into the hands of criminal gangs; this denial of legal avenues has created a flourishing trade in forged documents as well as dangerous routes to Europe, posing additional security risks in countries that have already suffered lethal terrorist attacks.

The Syrian refugee crisis is on a breathtaking scale but it will not be the last of its kind, demonstrating the urgent need for countries with a commitment to universal human rights to come up with a practical and humane plan for dealing with such emergencies. The EU was not set up to accommodate movements of millions of people in such a short span of time but its values require it to open its doors to people who need temporary refuge; we should not forget that most refugees never wanted to leave their homes and would like to return when it is safe for them to do so.

'I would not ask if conditions here would not force me to do all I can in time to be able to avoid worse,' Otto Frank wrote in his letter appealing for help from an American friend in 1941. Today his words apply as much to people desperately trying to escape the Assad regime in Syria or the murderous Taliban in Afghanistan. They are human beings, just like us, and they take such terrible risks only because they are trying *to avoid worse.*

Hubert Moore

CHANGE AT LEEDS

I can see you now.
You draw yourself up
to your full height, your best
South East English, to ask
a uniformed man at Leeds
about your connection to Bradford.

He shakes his head, tries
his Yorkshire accent on you.
You hardly catch a word.
Is it an exile's homing
instinct that you slip back
into sleep-talk and ask,

in Amharic, what platform
please for Bradford? And that
he, in sleep-talk too,
gives you platform-number,
time of departure, arrival-time
at Bradford, in Amharic?

FOR FIVE REFUGEES, ONE OF THEM A PIECE OF PAPER

I'm thinking that escape can't rest
until a journey back occurs, escaping
back. Ten years go past and then,
your citizenship, your passport
in your pocket, you take a boat
just like the one that carried you
across inside it (you were cowering
in a dustbin, you said) and ride it back,
stand on its deck like a mast.

And you and you and you, how
you must have cowered in the dark
hold of what they did to you,
their punching, entering, beating.
Somehow you stole off, coaxed that thing
up to a crack of light, allowed it
to have happened, spoke it, wrote it,
flew the fact of it as a flag in the wind.
You crossed back, you escaped.

And you, the ache for someone absent
written right-to-left on prison
notepaper, ten or twelve flimsy
lines – you slip out past the censoring
pen of guards at visiting-time.
Then, the scribble on the same
note's underside, you come back
escaping: the ache for someone else
who's absent, slipping back into prison.

Alex Wheatle
ALFRED AND VINCENT

It is said that many of the Wheatle men possess a large, squarish forehead and dark ebony, intense eyes. There is a short vertical line of determination that runs between their eyebrows. Their shoulders are what you can expect them to be following generations of manual labour and slavery. Their complexion is typically dark-chocolate. That was certainly true of my father, Alfred Alexander Wheatle, who was born in Old Harbour, Jamaica, in September 1933. He was the second son of Louis Charles Wheatle who had entered this unfair world in 1900. 'Charlie', as my grandfather was known, was a mysterious man. He seemed to have emerged from out of nowhere, arriving in Old Harbour as a very young man without a sixpence to his name and offering no clues as to where he grew up or his family resided. (I borrowed this intrigue for one of the major characters, Joseph Rodney, in my novel *Island Songs*.)

Some whispered my grandfather was descended from the maroons, journeying from Accompong Town, a small encampment in the remote interior of Jamaica that was named after a freedom fighter; runaway slaves had made their home there after they had waged war with the British Red Coats. Others *su-su'd* that Charlie simply came from the bush and would not elaborate any further.

Impressively tall and handsome, Charlie Wheatle was (unfortunately he didn't pass on his height to me). He walked the land with his strong, proud chin leading before him and his back was as straight as a Grenadier Guard's. He was a man of a few words but he had a kind smile. Nobody ever witnessed him losing his temper and he had a gentle nature about him. He never revealed his past or who he belonged to. Sometimes my father and his siblings would catch him unguarded peering into the north-eastern hills at sunset as if he was dwelling on some cruel memory, but whatever it was, he never said.

As the first shots were fired in the Great War, Charlie Wheatle journeyed to Old Harbour in the Jamaican parish of St Catherine. He won a job at the Government Bodles Agricultural Farm. He was put in charge of the water pump house and its maintenance. For over fifty years he rose at 4am, boiled a kettle on an open fire to brew his home-made coffee and strode uphill to his place of work carrying his kerosene lamp to guide him in the bush. He started his shift around 4.30am.

Charlie married a local girl named Whillel and they raised six children, three boys, three girls. My father Alfred, who they nicknamed Freddy, was the second born. Their house was no more than a two-room stone hut with an outside kitchen and pit toilet. On the land surrounding their humble dwelling, Charlie planted coffee, tobacco, cocoa, mango, ackee and a variety of vegetables. He suspended an old tyre from a branch for the children's entertainment and he would watch his *kidren* at play smoking his pipe of raw tobacco beneath the generous shade of a mango tree. Charlie was unwilling to raise a hand to discipline his offspring so Whillel had to serve out spankings when Freddy and his siblings were unruly. Despite his familiar surroundings, Charlie would never utter two words when one word would do.

Freddy attended the local school in Old Harbour where he was taught about the lineage of the British monarchy, sang songs about the all-conquering British Empire and learned that his supreme ruler was some white man living in a palace in faraway England. He also showed an aptitude for maths, technical drawing and woodwork. In fact, he had displayed enough promise for his parents to send him to a better-equipped school in the capital – Kingston School of Technology. This squeezed the family budget so Whillel, determined to see her favourite son receive a good education, sought part-time work as a cleaner and a cook. Freddy didn't mind rising before the roosters had crowed their first crow and arriving home when the cicadas had begun their evening chorus. He was very ambitious, wanting to one day design and build a home for himself with its own bathroom and toilet so his backside wouldn't be harassed by flies and other small things that buzzed, bit and hovered at night.

Possessing unusually long arms and skilled hands, Freddy excelled at his new school and graduated with full honours. His parents were very proud of him.

Soon after hostilities ended in the Second World War, white men from the UK landed in Kingston carrying clipboards, airs of superiority and Panama hats. They were representatives from British institutions including the newly formed National Health Service, the Post Office, British Rail and London Transport. On his way to visit a friend, fifteen-year-old Freddy spotted an Englishman sweating in his blazer, tie and black brogues at a downtown bar one Friday afternoon. Freddy hadn't seen too many white folks before so he took a chair near to where the white man was talking to a well-dressed, official-looking black man. The white man was smoking an English brand of cigarette and the Jamaican was puffing on a skinny roll-up. Both of them were drinking rum.

'We're looking for skilled tradesmen,' the white man said. 'No cowboys or butchers! We require proper certification from any man who applies. Cities in the UK need rebuilding. We need disciplined, hard-working men. Men who can easily mix and can laugh at the odd joke. They'll be paid extremely well and have a wonderful opportunity to live in the Motherland. God save the King! Those who are accepted can count themselves very lucky.'

Returning to Old Harbour the same night, Freddy told his parents about the white man in the bar. 'Cyan yu imagine, Papa? Me working inna Inglan'? Me could send you back ah money every week and yu could retire from de pump house and rest ya foot! When me come back me gwaan buil' myself ah big mansion wid *inside* toilets me ah tell yu!'

Charlie drew on his pipe and shook his head. 'And how do yu t'ink yu could travel to Inglan'? Swim? Me cyan't even afford to tek de bus to Mandeville and yu waan go ah Inglan'! Kiss me broad toe!'

For the next six years Freddy beseeched his parents about his dream of watching '*live and direct*' the monarch of England roll out of Buckingham Palace in a golden carriage. Whillel, keeping silent, would plead with her eyes but Charlie, offering no response, drew on his pipe and gazed into the hills.

By the end of 1953, Freddie had qualified as a carpenter and a draughtsman. He saved what money he could and he was determined to ride on a red London bus and plant his size eleven feet in London's Piccadilly Circus before his twenty-first birthday. Arriving home from work on a February evening in 1954 he spoke to his mother after dinner. 'Mama, me save up ah liccle money fe me fare to Inglan. Yu t'ink Papa could give me anyt'ing?'

A smile escaped Whillel's lips. 'Talk to ya papa,' she instructed.

Drawing on his pipe with his back against the mango

tree, Charlie was peering into the hills – the sun was dropping beyond the western ranges. 'Papa,' Freddy began nervously. 'Me save up all de money me cyan. Do... do yu t'ink yu could find ya way to give me ah liccle somet'ing to put forward to me fare to go ah Inglan'?'

Freddy studied Charlie's expression but could not guess his response. Rising to his feet, Charlie instructed, 'Follow me.'

He picked up a hammer from the outdoor kitchen before leading Freddy into the bedroom where Charlie slept with Whillel on a thin mattress. He raised the bedding and, using the hammer, drew up a floorboard. The gap in the floor revealed an old tobacco tin. Charlie wrenched off the lid and took out the wad of notes bound in an elastic band. He passed the cash to Freddy. 'When yu go, mek sure yu write to ya mama once ah mont'. If you nuh do dat she will cuss de morning, de chicken, de goat and everyt'ing else. So ***don't*** forget dat.'

There wasn't a prouder man in town when Freddy collected his British passport that was delivered to the Old Harbour post office in April 1954. He stared at his own photo and carefully thumbed through the pages. It was signed by the governor of Jamaica. 'The land of milk and honey and Buckingham Palace!' he whispered to himself.

He set sail from Kingston Harbour in June 1954. Whillel sobbed as the Italian-built ship disappeared over the horizon; Charlie had decided that the work at the pump house was more important than bidding farewell to his most ambitious son. His last words to Freddy were, 'Don't forget to write ya mudder. And remember, step like ah ***proud*** black man. Coromanty blood flowing t'rough yu.' They shook hands.

Led to his cabin by an Italian crew member wearing a white uniform, Freddy soon learned that the ship was already inhabited by Grenadians, Barbadians, St Lucians and other Caribbean islanders. Wary of them, Freddy kept company with his fellow Jamaican folk. Mento and calypso songs, backdropped by the sounds of dominoes slapping tables, echoed along the long corridors of the ship at night. The vastness of the seas scared him and the heaving waves made him sick. The night winds on deck froze his bones. The stars promised a prosperous future. Freddy couldn't help but laugh at the banter between the islanders in the canteen hall. 'Ya island is so damn small dat it nuh even big enough to hol' ah cricket match,' a Jamaican would say.

'And Jamaicans are so wild dat de slavemaster had to put dem on a leash whenever they go inside de big house!'

'Come say dat again and see if me don't t'ump yu down, smallie!'

'Jus' like ah Jamaican! Always ready for ah fight.'

'Jus' like ah dyam smallie! So quick to back off and bow! Yu tek to slavery like de English tek to tea and jam sandwiches!'

Missing his mother's cooking, Freddy just managed to keep down the spaghetti Bolognese the ship's crew cooked every other day. He made good friends and they all reaffirmed their belief in God during a violent sea storm.

Among the passengers were two stowaways – Vincent and Errol. Vincent had been an orphan from downtown Kingston – he had lost his mother when she gave birth to him. When he was five years old he had witnessed his father's murder in a dispute over the ownership of a chicken. Ever since that traumatic event he had been feeding off scraps and living off his wits in the Kingston ghettos. Errol was born in a one-room shack in the lush parish of St Mary. His mother died from diabetes when he was a child. His father placed him with aunts upon aunts and cousins upon cousins until they grew tired of feeding him. He didn't know his surname so he insisted it was *Flynn* after the Hollywood actor. He never attended school but harboured big dreams.

At the age of thirteen, Errol found himself a tiny strip of land where he began cultivating spring onions – locals called it scallion. But growing increasingly exasperated at trying to hustle a living selling vegetables at the local market, he hitch-hiked to Kingston to seek his fortune. He and Vincent became 'brothers'.

Freddy and his fellow compatriots took turns in taking down plates of food for Vincent and Errol. They slept on cabin floors and kept out of sight during the day. They had visions of returning to Jamaica in three piece suits, top hats and carrying shiny black walking canes.

'Yes, sah!' Freddy said to Vincent and Errol. 'An' me ambition is within two years to buil' ah nice place halfway up de Blue Mountains wid ah driveway. Me will have *two* toilets inside. Yes, mon! De breeze up der cyan cool yu off nice.'

The ship docked for a day in Genoa. Freddy and his friends explored the Italian port city. Below decks, Vincent and Errol plotted their escape from customs officials at the UK.

The night before their arrival in the UK, Vincent promised, 'Freddy! Tomorrow's de big day! Soon, we'll be drinking de queen's tea and smoking Embassy cigarettes in Brixton market.'

Blue skies and seagulls welcomed passengers onto English shores. Stripped to their vests and provisions strapped and taped to their backs, Vincent and Errol plunged into green-blue seas. For a few seconds their heads disappeared beneath the ripple and white trail of the ship. Watching their bodies resurface, Freddy said to himself, 'Me hope de cold water nuh kill dem both!'

Freddy stepped ashore in Southampton. Once they navigated customs, he and his friends searched the beaches for Vincent and Errol. They couldn't be found. Presuming them lost at sea, they mournfully trudged their way to the train station.

On their way, a white man, wearing a stained apron and

overalls, was sweeping a pavement. Shocked at this scene, Freddy checked his stride to take a closer look. All the Englishmen he had ever seen were garmed in nice suits, natty hats and black shoes. They smoked cigarettes from shiny cases. They never wore aprons.

'What you looking at, monkey-face?'

The smile evaporated from Freddy's face. He stood his ground and offered a fierce *eye-pass.*

'You want to make something of it, nigger?'

Before Freddy could react he was pulled away by his kin. 'Freddy! Simmer down! Yu waan to get arrested and tek de next boat back to Jamaica? What will yu say to ya mama and papa?'

On their journey to London, Freddy and his friends could not erase the image of Vincent and Errol's dive for raw opportunity. *Me should ah talked dem out of it,* Freddy rebuked himself. *We could ah reason wid de custom officials. We could ah helped dem fill in de necessary forms.*

The train pulled in to its final destination – Waterloo. Once Freddy had stepped off the locomotive, he had to stand still and take in his surroundings. Smoke fumed above his head. The loud speaker system blitzed his ears. People seemed to walk so fast like it was the last day of the world. What happened to the British *how do you do* and tipping your hat in greeting that he had seen in films? Here, no one knew him, nobody even acknowledged him unless in his confusion and wonder he stepped in someone's way. '*Get your arse out of my fucking way, nigger!*'

He eventually boarded a bus and headed for Brixton. He clutched his luggage close to his chest. He read the tobacco and soap advertisements painted above shops on brick buildings. He was almost hypnotised by the smoke spiralling out of untold chimneys. He wondered about the fate of Vincent and Errol. *Could they be alive? Did we search long enough? Did they know de right train that stops at Waterloo? Would they know de right number bus that'll take dem to Brixton?*

While seated, he read an address that he had written on a piece of paper. Getting off at Brixton High Street, Freddy approached pedestrians and asked for directions. Anybody white couldn't comprehend his accent. 'Can't understand your jungle language, mate!'

He was finally directed to Harbour Street, a road leading off Coldharbour Lane. He smiled at the coincidence of the street name. The landlady was a skinny Irish woman who owned more freckles on her face than Freddy could count. Her crucifix was swinging from her neck every time she moved her head. She showed Freddy to his third-floor box-room. 'I want a month's deposit. *No* parties, *no* women and certainly *no* bloody pets! The toilet's outside in the back yard. I run a clean household and you'll be out on your dark ears if you try to change that.'

Freddy peered out of the window and was relieved to see the toilet was housed in a small hut. He only had one question. 'Please, Miss, where is de employment exchange?'

'You'll have to go back to Brixton for that. Near the end of Coldharbour Lane. Next door to the laundry works.'

Starting work two days later renovating terraced housing that had suffered bomb damage, Freddy was quick to inform his supervisors that he knew how to construct the joints and angles to build roofs and staircases. He was competent at fitting sash windows and constructing wooden frameworks for walls. He understood concrete shuttering and foundation work and knew how to use a plumb line and set a building level. He also told them that he could read an architect's drawing and recognised all the symbols and terminology. 'You, Chalky?' a foreman laughed. 'You're having me on! Just keep stirring the cement.'

Following a working day, Freddy would follow his

work colleagues to a pub that was willing to serve black immigrants. Many didn't.

He noticed that the Irish and his fellow West Indians always had to wait to be served after the English, even if they were already at the bar and an Englishman had just walked in. Loose change was often tossed onto the counter or even on the floor following his purchase of a pint of Guinness. Fights would break out if a black man smiled at a white woman.

The reaction only got worse if Freddy and his friends ventured into the West End. More often than not they were refused entry. *'No fucking niggers! This is a respectable club! We don't want you near our women. Go on! Fuck off out of it!'*

Seven weeks later, Freddy found himself working on a building site in Camberwell. He was now trusted to hang doors, build walls and fit sash windows. At morning break, he recognised the broad-shouldered man making the tea. He was being very careful with the milk he dropped into the mugs. He stirred slowly, not wanting to spill a drop. Beneath his jacket he was wearing layers of sweaters. A cloth cap crowned his head. Next to him, a cement-stained spade was leaning against two breeze blocks. It was Vincent. Freddy rushed up to him. 'So yu make it!'

Vincent couldn't match Freddy's grin. 'Me try me best, Freddy. But me affe let him go. Errol never tell me he could nuh swim.'

Kate Clanchy
SHAKILA'S HEAD

Miss! Shakila slips from the shade behind the library, blinking in the Sports Day sun.

I wonder again what Shakila does to her hijab, and why it seems to sit fuller and higher than the other girls' – a Mother Superior hijab, or one from a Vermeer. It can't be starched. Maybe it's draped over twisted horns of hair, like Carrie Fisher's in *Star Wars*. That would go with her furry eyebrows, her slanting, sparking, black eyes, her general, Mongolian, ferocity.

Miss! cries Shakila, I won the 400 metres!

You did? Isn't it Ramadan? Aren't you fasting?

Shakila nods. I still won. And Miss! I'm coming to Poetry Group. After the hurdles. Here. Poem.

She hands me a sheet of A4, and dashes back into the playing field. It is 28 degrees and getting hotter. Under her rugby shirt and long trousers, Shakila grows thin.

The poem, though, is very fine: a variation on a theme I gave the group last week, contrasting the morning Adhan from the mosque in her native Afghanistan with the alarms of her new life in England. I'm more interested, though, in the writing on the other side of the sheet, which she has crossed out suspiciously neatly so the whole text is still visible and begging to be read. It's about a man sweating, and a scarf and a backpack and suspicious minds – so when, because of Sports Day, just Lily and Priya turn up to Poetry Group, I ask her about it.

Oh, she says, I was trying to write, you know, about terrorists.

What about terrorists?

But I couldn't make it work. Miss! It was too hard.

Terrorists here? In this country?

I'm assuming the poem is a protest against suspicion of Muslims in Britain. I'm aware there are a group of Afghans in the neighbourhood now. The local café has a new name, and a map of Afghanistan on the wall, and you can now order a whole sheep, twenty-four hours in advance. I got in a discussion with the cook about the poet Rumi. He looked just like Shakila, come to think of it, so maybe—

No, Miss, says Shakila, eyes snapping, ivory fingers blossoming in scorn. In England? There are no terrorists in England.

She's from Afghanistan, says Lily, she means the Taliban.

Lily is an alternative type, a Goth with heavy eyeliner who always knocks about with the black girls: nevertheless, I assume this is a white stereotype, and I am about to correct her when Shakila nods, more vehement than ever.

Miss! I am Huzara people.

Like *The Kite Runner*, says Lily, glancing at me smugly.

I don't know, says Shakila.

It's a book, I say, about Afghanistan. It's on the A Level, isn't it, Lily?

The Taliban, says Shakila, hate us. When my mum went to get our visa, Miss, the bus was bombed, not her bus, but the one in front. Miss! I thought she would never come home.

But, says Lily, I thought you were Muslim? She offers me a Monster Munch. Usually, at Poetry Group, Shakila brings us cherries and strawberries, shining like the roses in her cheeks. She and Priya are pale today.

I am Muslim, says Shakila, I am Shia.

What's that? asks Lily. I raise an eyebrow. Clearly, this wasn't in *The Kite Runner*.

A different kind of Muslim, I fill in. Like Protestant and Catholic.

The Taliban hate the Shia, says Shakila, flatly. They kill us, all the time.

Priya leans across the table. Her dress is to the floor, her hijab is soft, striped and biblical, her teeth in braces, her face, as so often, full of delicate feeling. She is from Bangladesh, originally, a Sunni.

Miss! she says, but she is talking to Shakila. When I found out about that, when I learned that there were other kinds of Muslim, I didn't believe it. I said to my teacher in the mosque, this is not true, how can this be?

There is only one Koran, says Shakila. There is only one Allah.

Priya says: Miss! Don't laugh. When I was a little girl I thought the television was true. I mean, the black and white. I thought the past was black and white, Miss, I thought England was black and white. When I found out about Shia and Sunni, it was like that for me – I mean, when I found I was wrong.

You should write that down, says Lily, this is Poetry Group. How old was you when you came here, Priya?

Six – Priya often writes about it. Beautiful poems.

Me, I was fourteen, says Shakila—

Sunni, Shia there is no difference really, says Priya. Just – some prayers. Wait – do you whip yourselves?

No! snorts Shakila. I mean, not really. It is a – thingy. A symbol. She leans her hijab to Priya's hijab, puts her hands across the table. You know, she says, in my country, they caught this terrorist, this bomber, they put him on television, he said he was doing it for the Taliban, but he didn't know anything, he did not know – and she breaks into Arabic, sharp and triumphant – Ash-hadu Allah ilaha illallah!

Ash-hadu anna Muhammadar rasulah! chimes in Priya, both girls bow their heads.

What's that? asks Lily, and Shakila gazes at her.

A prayer, she says, one that everyone knows.

Except the Taliban fighter didn't know it, I say. Or not with a gun to his head.

But, says Lily, this bloke, the Taliban bloke on the telly, was he the same as in this poem?

No, says Shakila. This was another one—

Priya raises her head: How can a Muslim hate another Muslim? Miss! It is terrible, Miss.

A real terrorist? says Lily. In your poem? Like, you met him?

Yes! says Shakila. I saw him in the street – in the market, and I had this feeling, he is wrong. He is sweating, he wears all these clothes.

What clothes?

Like, you know, jacket, big thingy. Scarf, big trousers. It is hot, it is summer, I had a feeling, run away, run away from this guy. I catch my friend's hand. We run.

Yes, says Lily, but was he real? A real terrorist?

Yes, says Shakila, real. I ran, I screamed, I ran, everyone ran. There was an explosion. I was hiding, behind a thingy. Wall. He was in a bomb. He exploded. You heard it. Boom.

And then the bell rings for a long time, and we flinch from its noise.

Priya says: You need a frame. For your poem. Miss. Give her a frame.

A frame. I have taught them this. Each week, we look at a literary shape, a form, a piece of rhetoric, and they try it out for themselves. I don't suggest what they might write about, just the way they might write it. A frame, I say every week. Try this frame. Never: tell me about... Certainly not: unload your trauma. And still, they tell me these terrible things.

Yes, says Shakila, a frame. How shall I say it, Miss?

I haven't the slightest idea. Shakila folds her hands on her bag, waits.

That, says Lily, was a really good discussion. We reckon we should have filmed it. Like for RE? I have to go.

And she goes. So does Priya, leaving me to search my mind for the right frame for a poem about recognising a terrorist in the marketplace and then running away.

Shakila says: Miss! You know, bombs. Miss, the worst thing is, they cut you. They cut off bits of you Miss, like your feet, your leg! And when the bomb goes off, Miss, those body parts they land in the town around.

Did that happen in that bomb? I ask. In your poem. Did you see that?

Miss, she said, when I was in the place, behind the wall. A head came over. A whole head.

His head? I ask. The terrorist's?

Just, she says, you know, a head. In a scarf. A woman. A head.

Right, I say. I look at the sunlight coming in the slats of the blinds and I suggest that the interrogative mood might be good for poems like this, and short lines probably, and regular stanzas. A ballad, perhaps, or a set of instructions. How to recognise a terrorist. Shakila says she will send me the poem, by email.

And she leaves. I sit and stare, listen to the roar of the children finding their classrooms, the silence as the doors close and the register is taken. This is an orderly school, I remind myself. A just one. A safe one. As Lily said, it is beautiful to see Shakila and Priya extend hands across the table. More people should know.

Then I think I will go to the staff room, and find someone to tell. There will be someone there, someone to listen and to counter with some equally horrifying tale, and we will rehearse all the interventions available, all the help school extends, which is good help, the best available anywhere, the best anyone can do. We will remind each other this is why we work here, why our school does so well. Our multicultural intake, our refugee pupils, so colourful, so very often brilliant, so, in the modern parlance, vibrant.

But it won't do any good. Here in my ears is the sound of a bomb, a home-made one, a glass and fertiliser one, in a small town in Afghanistan, and it sounds like the school bell. And here on the desk beside me, disguised as a sheet of A4 paper, is a head cut off at the neck, its eyes shut, its blood stains minimal, like John the Baptist on a plate. Shakila's head, in its elaborate hijab, for how else am I to picture the Huzara people, Persian speakers, Genghis Khan's soldiers, lovers of Rumi, other than as my dear Shakila, my difficult, vehement pupil? Does she feel the lighter of it, I wonder, now it is me who has to carry the head home? Or will it be equally heavy, however often it is passed, just as much a head? Well, we can find out. Shakila's head: the weight of it, the warmth. Here you are. Catch.

Tim Finch

A REFUGEE'S STORY

This is the story of a policy analyst, a campaigner, and a journalist. They all worked on refugee issues. The policy analyst said, what's the solution? The campaigner said, what's the message? The journalist said, what's the story?

It is also the story of a writer.

The writer said, what's the story?

That's what I said, said the journalist.

So you did, said the writer. What I should have said is, what's *her* story?

Her story? said the campaigner and the policy analyst. Who's she?

Good question, said the writer. At this stage, I don't know.

Tell me about it, said the journalist. I'm always asking for her story, whoever she is. Stories like hers make all the difference.

Don't look at me, said the campaigner.

I'm looking at you because you could help me but you rarely do, said the journalist.

That's because her story is not just *a* story, it's her *life*, said the campaigner. It's not for me to tell it to you.

I don't want *you* to tell it to me, said the journalist. I want *her* to tell it to me.

And it's not for me to tell her to tell it, said the campaigner. To you or to anyone else. If she wants to tell it, fine. But if she doesn't...

No story, said the journalist.

You could make it up, said the writer.

No, you couldn't, said the journalist, laughing.

Sorry? said the policy analyst.

You couldn't make it up, said the journalist, still laughing.

Don't look at me, said the campaigner. The journalist was looking at her again.

What I mean is, *I* could, said the writer. Make it up, that is.

I couldn't, said the journalist. Could either of you? She was looking at the campaigner and the policy analyst.

No, I work with real people, true lives, said the campaigner, shaking her head.

Yes, I work with hard facts, the best evidence, said the policy analyst, nodding his head.

Four million Syrians, said the writer, that sort of thing?

Yes, that sort of thing, said the policy analyst.

And when you know that, what more needs to be said? said the campaigner to the writer.

Don't answer, let me, said the journalist to the writer. Four million Syrians is a number not a story.

No, it's a number that tells a story, said the campaigner.

Or begs a story, said the writer.

Tell me about it, said the journalist, laughing again.

The writer started reading from a book:

Do not misunderstand me: I would have closed my country to the likes of me if I were you. A journalist and poet of some distinction, I ask you! Do we not have enough of those already?

Your book? said the policy analyst, looking at the writer.

Yes, my book, said the writer.

But who are you to write her story in her voice? said the campaigner.

The writer of her story in her voice, that's who, said the writer.

But unlike her you're not a refugee, said the policy analyst.

Why would you assume, said the writer, that because I made up her story in her voice and she's a refugee, I am not a refugee?

Well, are you? said the journalist.

No, said the writer.

The other three all laughed.

But... said the writer.

We know... said the campaigner.

That is not the point, said the policy analyst.

And you are right, said the journalist, looking at the writer. The other two stopped laughing. The point is, said the journalist, an important story of a refugee has been told. Perhaps of one of the four million Syrians.

Who can all speak for themselves, said the campaigner.

Yes, and write what they choose to write, said the writer.

This is the story of a policy analyst, a campaigner, and a journalist...

The writer was reading from a book again. Or so it seemed.

That sounds familiar, said the policy analyst.

It's the start of her story, said the writer.

Her story? said the policy analyst.

Yes, the story she, a refugee, is writing about us, and her, said the writer. Because of course she is the writer here.

Oh, very clever, said the journalist.

Yes, said the campaigner. And I agree this writer, this refugee writer, must say, must write...

I don't like the word 'must' in this context, said the policy analyst.

Is at liberty to say, is at liberty to write... said the campaigner.

Thank you, said the policy analyst.

... what she wants, said the campaigner.

You said it, said the writer, smiling. Or rather, she had you say it.

Knowing that you would freely want to say it, said the journalist, laughing.

Which is all very clever, I agree, said the campaigner, not smiling or laughing. But is it what people want to hear, want to read, from a refugee writer especially?

Does that mean, said the writer, that the refugee writer should write:

My name is Nasrine, I am from Syria. They bombed my home. My family was killed. I was not safe, I had to flee.

Now you are mocking her, said the campaigner.

No, I am respecting her, said the writer. I am respecting her right as a writer to mock the idea that refugee writers must write like this, about that.

Or do you mean *she* is respecting *your* right as a writer etc., etc., said the journalist, because she's writing all this, right?

Oh please, said the campaigner.

It's one way of reading this story, that's all, said the writer. There are others.

But all this just seems like games, with form, with words, said the campaigner, when there's such an important story to tell.

Yes, a simple story simply told, said the policy analyst. I think that's the best way.

He's going to dispute the 'the', said the journalist. Just watch.

Yes, I am, said the writer. A simple story simply told is *sometimes* the best way. But as I said, there are other ways. I mean, how about if I introduce a musician and an artist into the story?

Must you? said the policy analyst.

No, said the writer.

But he has done, said the journalist.

They're both refugees, said the writer.

Are we? said the musician and the artist.

Who said that? said the policy analyst.

You could be, said the writer, looking at the musician and the artist. We all could be. At some stage.

But I'm from Brighton, said the artist.

Are you? said the musician.

Well, I am now, said the artist. I was born in Tehran.

Now you've lost me completely, said the policy analyst.

Yes, me too, said someone else.

Okay, let's say goodbye to the musician and the artist, said the writer.

Goodbye, said the musician and the artist.

Perhaps we could get back to the issue, said the journalist.

And to the facts, said the policy analyst.

Or at the very least, to her story, said the campaigner. I'd still like to hear it and doubtless the readers would too.

The *readers*? said the policy analyst and the journalist. There are readers?

Never mind them, said the writer.

Look, all I know, said the campaigner, is that this story is titled *The Refugee's Story*.

How do you know that? said the policy analyst and the journalist.

See the top of page 1, said the writer.

The policy analyst and the journalist flicked back to the top of page 1. Ah, yes.

Oh, this is hopeless, said the campaigner.

I'm sorry, said the writer. Perhaps you're right. Perhaps her story, *The Refugee's Story*, would have been better if it had been more conventional.

I bet the editor would have preferred that, said the journalist, laughing.

There's an *editor*? said the writer.

There's always an editor, said the journalist. But this

refugee writer of yours wouldn't be much of a writer if she worried about that.

True, said the writer. But she isn't, as you put it, 'this refugee writer of mine'. She's a refugee writer in her own right. Or rather, a *writer* in her own right. And at some point she is going to have to...

What? said the campaigner and the policy analyst.

I was going to say 'submit', said the writer.

Oh, I wouldn't say that, said the campaigner and the policy analyst laughing.

Hand over? said the writer.

A little better, said the campaigner and the policy analyst.

But hasn't she faced much worse? said the journalist. The state censors, the secret police.

I'm starting to get into this, said the policy analyst.

It's coming to life, I grant you, said the campaigner.

Should I not press send then? said the writer.

'Press send', yes, that's it, said the campaigner and the policy analyst.

And before the journalist could say, I think it should be her decision, the writer had pressed send.

Elaine Feinstein
THE OLD COUNTRY

In memory of my grandfather, Menachem Mendl

Do we inherit fear in the stories of
borders and slippery mud on river banks,
bribes and guards and angry dogs?
My grandfather always spoke of Odessa
with love: the music in street cafés,
acacia trees, and summertime
on Deribasovskaya.

He ran away from conscription
in the hated Tsar's army – but
carried poetry and homesickness
in his heart as he made for England
'the country of fair play'
as he always taught me.

A cheerful man into his old age –
he lived in our front room during the war –
reading the *News Chronicle* and Yiddish newspapers.
He was never afraid. I watched him shrug off
even the approach of his own death.
Wherever I learned fear, it was not from him.

FAR OUTSIDE THE CITIES

In Ukraine a woman who could be my ancestor
boils forest roots. She is shrivelled by winter.
Old at 42. Her husband went to fight invaders
and there is no news of him.
Diphtheria and typhus ravage
what is left of the village.

From my Western comfort I pity her harsh life,
though angels walk beside her
and her husband – no longer angry
and redeemed from vodka –
is waiting for her on the far shore
of a world we no longer believe in.

Noo Saro-Wiwa

A TIME TO LIE

I have never been a refugee. The closest I have come to that feeling (and it was not remotely close) was the night I spent near JFK Airport in New York. Flying in from London, my connecting flight to New Orleans didn't depart for another seven hours. Unwilling to spend money on a hotel, I decided to camp out overnight at Jamaica subway station in Queens.

The station had a cheap, all-night restaurant. Hip hop music pounded from speakers behind the bar – not the kind of hip hop I love but the nasty kind that doesn't cross the Atlantic, its futile lyrics bludgeoning me as I watched the world go by. The non-American travellers pulled wheelie suitcases. Most were in shape and exuded prosperity and hope. They were easily distinguishable from the locals, some of whom lolled past on creaking knees, their trans-fat complexions radiating ill-health. In a country where healthcare is at a premium, these residents of Queens were the discarded residue of the American-Dream-Melting-Pot. They looked as poorly maintained as New York's decrepit subway system. I started to wish I had splashed out on a hotel room.

The legs of my plastic chair and table screeched against the floor as I shifted about, trying to stay awake amongst this neon netherworld, so bright yet somehow dark. At 4am, the cleaners cordoned off the toilets for one hour. My bladder ached. When I was finally allowed to use the bathroom, two successive occupants of the cubicle beside me farted explosively before expressing their relief with loud sighs and murmurs ('Aaahh, yeah'). Culture shock can occur in the most unexpected places.

Back at my café table, I was mourning the death of my phone and laptop batteries. Without any internet to connect me to friends and family, I was bereft, a non-entity. The fact that I was only twelve hours away from meeting my friend and enjoying an expenses-paid vacation in Louisiana was immaterial – on that particular evening I was the loneliest person on earth.

Travel can do that to you. Being in a foreign place where others control your movements can sap your spirits and make you anxious, even under the most innocuous of circumstances. Remember the refugee crisis in Europe in 2015? 'It was the worst journey of our lives,' one woman told the BBC, her words plastered across its homepage. But she wasn't an African who had crossed an ocean of baked Saharan sand. Nor was she one of the millions of Syrians riding the Mediterranean waves on dinghies to escape Islamic State. This lady was a British holidaymaker, and she had been delayed for four hours on a Eurostar train en route to Paris. The train had ground to a halt after a group of asylum seekers broke out of Sangatte refugee camp and tried to enter the carriages.

The sound of their footsteps scampering on the roofs of the trains was understandably alarming to the British woman and her fellow passengers. But in the context of a refugee crisis that saw child corpses washing up on beaches, the lady's 'worst-journey-on-earth' was very much a First World Problem. Yet, if she could feel so rattled on that Eurostar train, and I could feel so depressed at a subway station in New York, then asylum seekers are clearly going through relative – and absolute – hell.

Yet sympathy for them is running dry in some quarters

of Britain. It is a curious paradox that although we live in an age in which every global tragedy and event is recorded, some people are trying to diminish the suffering of others more than ever. Asylum seekers are seen as liars, vectors of disease or religious fanaticism; economic 'migrants' who are capitalising on war to enjoy the benefits of life in the UK.

Their tenacity – a virtue in most other contexts – can only reflect a dangerous furtiveness and malevolence. This culture of disbelief permeates immigration officials' dealings with asylum applicants. Presumed liars until proven otherwise, they are prodded, tested and quizzed like crime suspects. And sometimes they give false stories and are exposed. Does this make them undeserving of asylum? Roberto Beneduce doesn't think so.

I met Beneduce during a recent trip to Italy. A professor of Medical and Psychological Anthropology in Turin, Beneduce has researched and spent time with Africans who have sought asylum in Italy. In his 2015 paper 'The Moral Economy of Lying', Beneduce discusses why some asylum seekers give incorrect information on their applications.

There are deep psycho-cultural fault lines that separate European immigration officials and African asylum seekers. For the immigration official, written bureaucracy is an organised system, the cultural norm. There is an assumption that certain data sources define and prove a person's identity. But the asylum seeker who is raised in a country with fragile public institutions and civil registry apparatus might not have the required documents. (I can attest to that bureaucratic fragility: my birth certificate, written somewhere in Port Harcourt, Nigeria, in 1976, is a flimsy piece of pink paper, the size of my palm. My details are written by hand, not even typed. As far as I know, this information is not stored on any computer. One day, when I can be bothered, I will scan the certificate and laminate it for preservation.)

Other Africans, especially those born in rural areas, may not know their precise date of birth. What are 'July' and 'August', anyway? A span of thirty days, named after a couple of Roman emperors from way back. What do such dates mean to the rural, fifty-something African? ***Uncle tells me I was born just after the rains started.*** The asylum seeker might pluck their birth date out of the air as their biro hovers above the blank space on a form. Their sense of identity is not wedded to birth certificates or utility bills. But without these details and supporting documents, the asylum seeker is a non-person in the eyes of the immigration official. They don't exist. Their suffering is a fiction.

The flimsy relationship between Third World identities and documentation was apparent in Algeria during colonial times. French administrators at prisons and government offices struggled to transcribe the myriad vowels in Arabic names. Consequently, they stopped trying to write down prisoners' names. Fingerprints were used instead: it's not easy shoehorning one's bureaucracy into a different culture.

The asylum seeker born out of shoddy bureaucracy often struggles to prove not only their identity but their ill-treatment too. The policemen who dragged them into African prison cells don't always fill out paperwork. Those same police might not maintain records of a gang rape reported to them by a distraught girl.

Gang rape is one thing, but what about the other types of suffering, the kind that may be considered ridiculous in the eyes of immigration officials? Some asylum seekers are fleeing ritual abuse, based on animist beliefs. The occult holds no currency in our empirical world, but the psychological terror imposed on its victims is real. And this terror can manifest itself in physical harm too.

What is the European immigration official to make of this? They are dealing with an asylum applicant who might talk about 'witchcraft' and ritual violence in a 'dreamlike language that challenges the bureaucratic grammar of human rights,' as Beneduce says.

The Istanbul Protocol guidelines for documenting torture stipulate that applicants must provide details – 'supplementary truths' – of horrific events. Can the asylum applicant necessarily retain such specifics? Traumatic flashbacks are often stored in fractured pieces in the brain. Having to unravel and verbalise these painful memories can re-traumatise victims, their asylum application playing out like a dangerously ad hoc psychotherapy session. When applicants are disbelieved by the immigration authority and sent back, it can be a huge psychological blow.

From the immigration official's perspective, there are questions as to why these applicants, having been arrested and beaten, can escape or are released so suddenly, yet are able to pass through airports unchallenged. How is it, the officials ask, that the applicant is arrested and hounded, yet their relatives are okay? But that's often how it works in Africa. Take my family, for instance: my father, a human rights activist, was executed by Sani Abacha's military regime in 1995. One of my cousins was arrested during that era of military rule. He was thrown into a jail so crowded there was only standing room. There were no regular showers, so the prisoners kept clean by caking their bodies with talcum powder. That cousin won asylum in the United States. Yet throughout that period of the 1990s, my father's youngest brother was a (legitimate) serving officer in the Nigerian army.

Some may find this hard to understand, this selective persecution. Oppression is supposed to be Rwandan-style, the baddies trawling death nets systematically across society, collecting victims and converting them into mountains of cadavers. There's a half-expectation that an atrocity will leave a trail of evidence, the Nazi dossier containing stock counts of Jewish tooth fillings. But Africa is a landscape dotted with patches of quicksand. You can walk for miles untroubled before suddenly falling in.

There is an idealised perception of what an asylum seeker looks like, and the legal criteria for refugees often correspond with that 'ideal'. Whether an individual asylum seeker fits that 'ideal' may vary from year to year. Although the pain of rape or torture may be constant and objective, the asylum process can be subjective, its criteria varying from country to country: violence in one country is deemed a 'crisis', while violence in another is not accorded the same status. This can confuse applicants. It makes as much sense to them as their supernatural rituals do to the European officials. Unsurprisingly, some asylum applicants change their stories, tell 'innocent lies', for fear that their particular ordeal won't pass muster.

'And,' Beneduce says in his research paper, '... what is the experience of those who, by telling the simple truth, see their request for asylum refused? This is the question that Omar – a young Malian who arrived in Italy at the end of 2010 – kept asking me, while scenes of persecution and death, ghosts of witchcraft and "voices from a satellite" tormented him unceasingly: "If I had said I was from Ivory Coast, as a guy suggested on the boat that took us to Lampedusa, they would have believed me, I would not be here. Instead, I am still here, with no job, without a thing! Oh Doctor, this does not work."'

And so the woman who has been gang raped by soldiers will point to her caesarean scar and pretend it is a stab wound. Such 'mendacity' strikes the cynic as a sign of immorality, a cause for deep suspicion. And this cynicism can reach laughable levels.

Take, for example, the Kenyan writer Binyavanga Wainaina. When he publicly declared his homosexuality in 2014, one British newspaper online commenter wrote: 'shall we be expecting at least one application for asylum shortly, then?'

A cursory Google search would have informed this commenter that Wainaina is the director of the Chinua Achebe Center for African Literature and Languages at Bard College in upstate New York. The Kenyan author crosses the globe attending literary and cultural events. He enjoys a purposeful and rich life. He doesn't want to live a jobless life in a British council house, watching TV re-runs of *Judge Judy*. In the commenter's mind, however, every African is an economic exploiter; Africans are neither fleeing persecution nor living satisfying lives. All truth is refracted through this prism of self-contentment.

The rise and fall in nations' fortunes is not a reflection of their people's superiority or inferiority. If, on the day Christ was nailed to a cross, someone had told a Roman consul that within two thousand years Albion (a small, damp island in north-west Europe) would rule a fifth of the world's land mass, the Roman would have thought that person was insane. The world evolves in ways we never foresee. Today's paradises could become the purgatories of tomorrow. Which is why it's best to treat others the way we would like them to treat us.

Seeking asylum is a lonely and painful process. Migrations of this sort are often considered a sacrifice. Most people don't want to leave their family, friends and culture any more than the Scottish crofters wanted to leave the Highlands during the eighteenth- and nineteenth-century clearances. These refugees may be the designated migrant. The rest of the family may have pooled their savings so that this individual can 'get out there', so to speak, and create a lifeline that makes the rest of the family's lives more bearable. Some parents can't bear to see their children suffering in a war-torn country. Better to send them on a journey to a safer region than have them hunker down in hell. It is a fraught and lonely experience for the migrant, a transition from frying pan to fire. These decisions are never taken lightly. The language around asylum seeking is indicative, as Professor Beneduce points out:

> 'In Lingala (the main spoken language in Democratic Republic of Congo) asylum seekers are called ***ngunda,*** literally "jungle", but in a wider sense the word also means "perdition". The whole process of escape to Europe is called ***kobwaka nzoto,*** ("to sacrifice", "to give up one's own body.") Bitumba noted a further meaning for the expression ***bwaka nzoto*** ("hand-me-downs") [cit. in Ayimpam 2014:91]. Different ideas coalesce in various expressions: dip into the water, sell off your body, sell off your identity (by using the name of someone other), use your body and exploit it even in dirty work, cheat... [Ayimpam 2014:90]... It is no coincidence that the loss of identity (as lived for example in the diasporic experience where one, often literally, becomes a non-identity, a *sans papiers*) is referred to in terms of a bodily loss (***kobwaka nzoto)*** [De Boeck and Plissart 2004:239]. Changing name, inventing a story, disavowing your birth-town, or your age, constitute a painful process, perceived as both a necessary tactic and a dispossession with little possibility of redemption.'

Migration is a complex issue. People will always disagree on intake numbers and overall policy. But whatever your position, we should never forget that they are human beings in fragile circumstances, and they deserve our respect.

William Boyd
THE DEATH OF KEN SARO-WIWA (1941–1995)

These two pieces, one written in 1993 (and never since republished) and the other in 1999, form a baleful narrative that charts the tragic end of a friendship I enjoyed and relished with the Nigerian writer and activist Ken Saro-Wiwa. In any human existence, historical forces will inevitably touch our lives, sometimes tangentially or, if we're unlucky, with full force. In my own life, for example, I have known fatal victims of IRA terrorism (the Harrods bomb of 1983) and Libyan (the Pan Am Flight 103 Lockerbie disaster in 1988) but I never, ever, in my darkest imaginings, thought I could ever know anyone who would be tried and executed by the state.

Ken Saro-Wiwa and I met in the mid-1980s initially as two writers who had Nigeria in common. He was an extraordinary dynamo of a man and I wrote an introduction to his masterwork, his novel about the Nigerian civil war, *Sozaboy*. Moreover, Ken had known my father, Dr Alexander Boyd, when Ken was a student at Ibadan University. But I saw in the early '90s how he was becoming radicalised by what was happening to his tribal homeland in the Niger delta, polluted by the international oil companies drilling for oil there – notably Shell Oil. I remember him telling me how he was trying to have his people, the Ogoni, recognised by the UN as a registered and threatened minority in Nigeria.

It was a perverse compliment to the effect of his political agitation that, in 1993, he was arrested in Nigeria and held without charge. I had a letter from him – smuggled out of jail – asking if there was anything I could do to help get him released. This first article was published by *The Times* in the summer of 1993.

The Arrest and Detention of Ken Saro-Wiwa

I came back from holiday to discover that a friend of mine had been arrested. This was a first, but matters soon degenerated further. My friend had not been arrested by the police, but by the state. Furthermore, no charges had been made against him and he was being held incommunicado. The name of my friend is Ken Saro-Wiwa and the government that has incarcerated him is that of Nigeria, head of state General Babangida.

Saro-Wiwa is an extraordinary man and an extraordinary writer. Indeed, I can think of no other writer anywhere else in the world who reproduces even half of his many facets. He is a novelist and a writer of children's books. He is a publisher who publishes and distributes his own works and those of other Nigerian writers. He is a campaigning journalist, of uncommon vigour, whose weekly columns over the years – in the Nigerian newspapers the *Vanguard* and the *Sunday Times* – possess a *saeva indignatio* and uncompromising vitriol of which Jonathan Swift would be proud. On top of these attributes he is the financier, producer and writer of a soap opera on Nigerian television called *Basi & Co* which, I believe, holds the world record for the most watched soap opera ever, with upward of 30 million viewers – one out of three of Nigeria's 90 million plus population sitting down to watch at any one time.

What makes *Basi & Co* more than just an astonishing ratings success is the fact that it does not purvey some fantasist's notion of suburban angst or some whimsical version of middle brow wish-fulfillment. Rather it concerns itself with the get-rich-quick scams of its down and out hero Basi and his cronies, and their inevitable and remorseless failure, creating thereby a potent indictment of personal apathy and the graft-obsessed attitude that Saro-Wiwa considers has infected and corrupted Nigerian society. *Basi & Co* has a genuine moral fervour behind it, an attempt through satire to encourage Nigerians both to laugh at themselves and to mend their ways.

Saro-Wiwa wants his country to improve itself. He wants its citizens to work hard and excel and fill out a role in Africa and the world that Nigeria should be occupying. His own life exemplifies the virtues he prescribes. Born in 1941 near Port Harcourt in the east of Nigeria on the Niger River delta Saro-Wiwa was educated at the University of Ibadan where he read English literature. When the Nigerian civil war broke out in 1968 he was trapped in the secessionist east – Biafra – but managed to escape and crossed the front lines to the federal side. He was appointed civilian administrator to the crucial oil port of Bonny, a post he held for the rest of the war.

Although an easterner, Saro-Wiwa did not support the Biafran cause because it was dominated by the Ibo tribe. As an Ogoni (one of the thirty or so significant ethnic groups that the Ibos had corralled into Biafra) Saro-Wiwa felt that an Ibo-dominated Biafra was not in his people's best interests. This concern for the rights of the Ogoni people within a federal Nigeria remains the cause closest to his heart and it is his recent efforts on their behalf that, as far as one can gather, have led to his arrest.

The homelands of the Ogoni lie on top of Nigeria's oil

resources. The extraction of petrochemicals by multinational oil companies has devastated the countryside and produced no revenue at all for the people on whose land the reserves have been found. Over the last few years Saro-Wiwa has campaigned with his usual unremitting vigour for justice and reparations for what he describes as the progressive 'genocide' of his tribe. Saro-Wiwa has been scathing in his accusations directed both at the oil companies and at Babangida's government, he has taken his case to the UN and organised a peaceful demonstration of 300,000 people in Ogoniland in January this year. Somebody obviously decided he should be stopped.

Saro-Wiwa is a brave man and a force for good in Nigeria. Everything he has achieved in his writing and professional life has been undertaken with the view of improving the lot of his countrymen and releasing their potential. He writes for a Nigerian audience, he publishes for Nigeria, he campaigns in his journalism against corruption and stupidity and he struggles to achieve justice for oppressed Nigerian minorities. When a state arrests and holds without charge citizens of this calibre it is a sign of terminal decay. President Clinton and the US government are reassessing their position regarding Nigeria in the light of the annulled democratic elections last month. It's to be hoped that John Major's government will follow suit. If the Nigerian government is concerned to reassure the world community of its essential probity then one of their first acts should be the unconditional release of Saro-Wiwa.

Ken was released and our occasional long lunches resumed. Then one day he told me he was going back to Nigeria. But this time he never returned.

The following piece was updated in 1999 from an article published in the *New Yorker* shortly after Ken's death in 1995.

* * *

I first met Ken Saro-Wiwa at a British Council conference in Cambridge in 1986. While he had been a student in the 1960s at the University of Ibadan, in western Nigeria, he had been treated by my late father who then was running the university's health services. Ken had recognised my father in the thinly disguised portrait of him in my first novel, *A Good Man in Africa* (he appears as 'Dr Murray'), and was curious to meet his son.

As a result of that meeting a strong friendship ensued. I wrote a profile of Ken for *The Times* and we took to having regular lunches whenever he was in London, usually at the Chelsea Arts Club, a place he came to relish. We talked about books and writing in the main – Ken was a prolific author: novels, plays, children's books, journalism, TV soap operas were all part of his oeuvre – and of course Nigeria, but I became aware as the 1990s arrived that an increasing radicalisation was taking place in him. It was all to do with oil and the despoliation of his tribal homeland – Ogoniland – in the Niger River delta by the multi-national oil companies – Shell in particular. The wanton disregard for ecological good-management had condemned the Ogoni people – whose livelihood was farming and fishing – to live in a pestilential circle of hell. The lush forests and the winding creeks of their homeland in the delta had been transformed by massive oil spills and 24-hour gas flaring into one of the most noxious and polluted places on earth. Ken was determined to do something about it and, with other Ogonis, created MOSOP – the Movement for the Survival of the Ogoni People. A highly organised, scrupulously non-violent protest campaign was initiated – and Ken's troubles began to multiply.

Nigeria was then ruled by a succession of corrupt military governments sustained, in every sense of the word, by the huge revenues that Nigeria's oil provided. Any protest movement, however internationally recognised, that threatened the flow of petro-dollars was in harm's way. Ken and MOSOP's agitation was proving highly successful – a fact measured by the amount of state persecution they attracted.

Ken endured a period of house arrest in 1992 but in June 1993 he was arrested again and jailed without charge (the period is recorded in his prison diary, published as *A Month and a Day*). I came back from my summer holiday that year to find a series of messages on my answer-phone from MOSOP organisers asking if there was anything I could do to help publicise Ken's ordeal. Amnesty International had made him an official 'Prisoner of Conscience' but MOSOP was finding it hard to keep up the pressure.

In the light of Ken's global posthumous fame it's perhaps worth recalling that in 1993 MOSOP and the Ogoni people's suffering was barely known abroad. The scandal of Shell Oil's heedless devastation of the Niger River delta hardly figured in the world's news bulletins. I decided to ask *The Times* if they wanted an article. The profile of Ken that I had written had been a lavish multi-page colour spread in the magazine. I thought the newspaper might be intrigued to learn that their interviewee was now languishing in a noisome jail in Port Harcourt. Here, Peter Stothard, then editor of *The Times*, came to our aid. He commissioned the piece and ran it with due prominence in the paper. It was sufficiently obvious to attract the attention of BBC Radio 4's *Today* programme. I was invited on one morning and spoke about Ken, the fact that he was in jail and about MOSOP's campaign against the Nigerian military and multi-national, all-powerful oil companies. The military dictator at the time was General Ibrahim Babangida. Babangida – the name is resonant – was mentioned a great deal in the conversation on air.

Ken was released on 22 July, free to return to the UK. I claim no credit for myself – many people were agitating for Ken's release at the time and indeed it was the decision by the editorial teams at *The Times* and *Today* to run the story that really swung things our way. The media events surrounding the case of Ken in July 1993 – an article in a national broadsheet and a primetime broadcast on BBC Radio – have always seemed to me to illustrate the positive power of unwelcome publicity. If there's a lesson to be learned it is that the key media outlets in this and any other country – those with the highest profile and influence – have an additional responsibility in the field of human rights as well: they are not simply there to report – they would be astonished at the significant difference they can make.

This point was reinforced when I saw Ken again in London and he told me a story – which must remain apocryphal as it can never be verified. He had been told, so rumour had it, that General Babangida's wife was in London at the time of the article and the broadcast, on a discreet but spendthrift shopping spree. Mrs Babangida had been shocked and alarmed to hear her husband's name mentioned blithely and without contradiction as a despot and a criminal on the BBC (and ashamed of the guilt by association) and had urged him to release this Saro-Wiwa man immediately. True or false, the anecdote does illustrate how a little bit of notoriety and press publicity can go a long way. I'm also sure, in this case, that the fact it was *The Times* of London and the British Broadcasting Corporation added to the perceived heft of the condemnation we were bandying about. Subsequently, in future agitations on Ken's behalf, as his situation became progressively more dire, *The Times* and *Today* proved the most loyal of supporters of MOSOP and the Ogoni cause, something Ken recognised and was always grateful for.

It is the bitterest irony that when Ken was arrested again, accused of murder in a kangaroo court, was condemned to death and eventually executed in 1995 the cries of outrage were both loud and universal in the world's media but proved ultimately powerless. Ken Saro-Wiwa, MOSOP and the ecological devastation caused by Shell were on everyone's agenda by then. But in Nigeria Babangida had gone, replaced by another general – Sani Abacha – whose cocaine-fuelled paranoia, fear and ignorance overrode all political pragmatism. Ken and his eight co-accused were hung on the morning of 10 November 1995. I genuinely believe that had Babangida still been in power Ken would have been reprieved but to some corrupt, warped minds no amount of press exposure makes a difference. Abacha himself – the most ardent and wholesale plunderer of Nigeria's state coffers – died less than three years later in highly suspicious circumstances. He may well have been poisoned by one of the Egyptian or Indian prostitutes he consorted with – and his tiny footnote in history will be his wilful, criminal responsibility for the unjust and lamented death of Saro-Wiwa, a real and actual good man in Africa. It is little consolation.

It's somewhat astonishing for me today to realise that it's almost exactly twenty years since Ken was executed by the Nigerian military government. The military no longer rule Nigeria, though Ogoniland is still grievously polluted. MOSOP still exists and the struggle continues. Shell has agreed to pay reparations to the Ogoni people and Saro-Wiwa is recognised globally as a selfless martyr to a noble cause. I think he would be surprised at the way his legacy and example have endured. Perhaps the greatest thing that can be said about him, twenty years on, is that he did not die in vain. That is some consolation.

Rose Tremain

Excerpt from

THE BEAUTY OF THE DAWN SHIFT

This story takes place after the fall of the Berlin Wall.

Two days later, Hector and his bicycle and his knapsack were helped into a truck and driven to Poznan station. Katarzyna scrubbed the room the German had vacated with a disinfectant so strong it made her teeth sting.

Hector S. was put into a freight car full of cauliflowers. 'I am sorry,' said the train driver, 'to put you with vegetables, sir.'

After this, there was just the dark of the freight car and the sound of all the miles and miles of the Polish heartland moving under the train. Hector lay down and covered himself with his overcoat, and was as still as a man can be on a bed of cauliflowers. His head and body ached, and it seemed to him that this ache was right in the substance of his skull and in the marrow of his bones.

His future was going wrong. Every thought that came to him, instead of being clear and precise, was clouded and difficult. It was as though thoughts were harmful chemicals, setting off explosions in his brain. The train was taking him nearer to his destination, but he began to see, with embarrassment, that it was towards the old eternal

Russia of his imagination that he was travelling and that although he'd prepared quite well for his journey, he hadn't prepared at all for his arrival. When his D-Marks ran out, where and how was he to live? For a start, he spoke only a few words of the language. He knew the Russian word for 'now', but not the Russian word for 'tomorrow'. What kind of work could he find which allowed him to be totally silent?

Then a new thought came. The colour of its chemical felt white. It was a thought about silence and the new world, the world of the West, creeping east. Westerners were thieves of silence. They stole the quiet in a place and in the mind of a man, and replaced it with longing, just as they stole the mystery from a city by lighting it orange. Darkness and quiet were leaving the world. It was only a matter of time before the dawn wouldn't be the dawn any more, but some other computer-adjusted piece of time, with colours other than its own.

Hector felt pleased with this thought, not because it was an optimistic one, but because it seemed rational and not blighted by confusion, and so he said to himself that perhaps he was going all this way in search of the perfect silence. He'd imagined a wilderness, a birch grove, a lake, or at least, he'd imagined cycling or walking through this kind of landscape *on his way* to his future in Russia. But the truth was that the future had no location. He'd never got further with his own story than the lake. Now, he understood that he might never get further – ever. In all probability, the lake was his destination.

Hector sat up and tried to eat a pickled cucumber. He had no appetite for what remained of the tinned meat. He lay down again, liking the train now, soothed a bit by the train, as if the train were Elvira and Hector a child falling asleep on her lap, wrapped in her apron.

He didn't want to show his face in Warsaw. He knew he would be stared at and he couldn't abide the thought of meeting the stare of Polish women and girls.

He dreamed the place smelled of spun sugar, that there was dry rot in the old houses, that church bells kept ringing and ringing the hours, that pigeons continuously ruffled the air. He would fall ill again in such a place.

So he resorted to bribery. He offered DM10 to the train driver and asked him to put him in another freight going east to the border with Belarus or beyond.

The train driver took the money and looked at it and shook his head. 'Now from here in a freight train going east, you will die of cold, sir.'

'I'm used to the cold,' said Hector.

'Not this one. This is more cold.'

'Please,' said Hector.

So the money was paid and a second driver was found who agreed to take him in a night train carrying medical supplies to Minsk. Katarzyna's husband then performed his last act of generosity: he gave Hector the blanket he kept in his cab. 'In the cold night,' he said, 'cover your body, German man.'

Hector missed the cauliflowers. In this second freight car, piled with boxes, every surface was hard and in whatever way he lay down, Hector's bones hurt. He tried folding the blanket in three and lying on top of it. This was more comfortable and Hector was beginning to drift towards sleep when he opened his eyes and saw in the darkness the freezing cloud of his own breath lying over him like a ghost. In time, he would have breathed all the air in the box car and the ghost would be very large and attempt to make more room for itself by entering the cavities of his body and taking away his life.

The blanket smelled of oil and it was old and worn, but

there was still a little warmth in it. Hector stood up and wrapped himself round and round in it and lay down again on the boxes of pharmaceuticals. He imagined he was lying on glass syringes, as clear as ice.

The night would be so long. Poland, thought Hector, is a place where the nights have subdued the days and stolen half their territory. The bit of space left to the light is so pitiful, you just have time to cycle a few kilometres, buy some hard bread, pass a church where women kneel at open-air confessionals, hear a village band wearing hats with emperor's plumes play an ancient march, and then the dusk comes down, and it's futile to look forward to morning, because morning is so far away. It wasn't so mad, so completely foolish to imagine that here, on certain days, you could go into a post office, say, to buy a stamp, and that when you came out again with the stamp in your wallet, the day had given up hope and the words 'post office' had faded into the wall.

These thoughts made Hector remember the line of post boxes in the lobby of the apartment building in Prenzlauer Berg and how he'd imagined letters from Russia arriving there, letters which described an epic journey, an honourable arrival, a life built in a place where the structures of the old familiar world were still standing.

Now, in his freight car, wrapped in the train driver's blanket, as heavy snow started to fall, Hector began to compose in his mind a letter to Ute, to the sister he'd desired since the day, at the age of five, when she'd licked his penis in the bath. It might be, he thought, the only letter he would have time to think up, and so he wanted it to describe a place that would seduce Ute, a place in which she would recognise that she could be happy, a place he had made safe for her in advance.

Dear Ute,
I have arrived at the loneliest, most beautiful place in the world. Let me describe it to you. It is a great forest that has been growing silently for more time than anything else on this part of the earth. Bears inhabit it. And reindeer and wolves. Snow lies over it for seven months of the year. Sometimes, I fall into conversation with a solitary hunter and we discuss weapons and the individual characteristics of flight of certain difficult targets and how, in one's aim, one may compensate for these and so kill after all and not starve. Bears are protected and may not be shot.

And this brings me to swans. At the feet of the forest is the lake. The north side of it is frozen, but a little water still laps the snow on the southern side and here I have discovered a fine family of your favourite birds. They whoop like cranes in the early morning. They're plump and sleek from the quantity of fish they find in the lake. They are as tame as Karl and will come if I call them and feed from my hand. When you join me here, this is the first thing we will do: go down to the lake and visit the swans.

I expect you're wondering where we're going to live and how we're to find shelter. 'Hecti,' I hear you say, 'are you asking me to make love to you in the snow?' No, Ute. No, I'm not. Unless you want to do that.

I have found, at the lakeside, an old grey dacha, built of wood, with a stone chimney and a steep shingled roof. I walked into it like that girl in the fairy story and sat down in the largest of chairs. I found a smoked ham hanging inside the chimney. I found a larder full of apples. I found folded sheets for the bed.

It's as if this dacha was designed with me in mind, with everything necessary for my survival: an axe to chop wood, a fire to cook on, even a feather-bed

> *quilt for the nights, which are as cold as nights on the moon. So now, I'm able to say to you, don't waste any more time, sell whatever you have to sell – Elvira's hairbrushes, father's cache of cigarettes – and take the next train out of Berlin going east...*

It was at this point in his imaginary letter that Hector was jolted forwards and almost fell off the ledge of boxes on which he was lying. The train had stopped.

Hector listened. He hadn't seen the thick snow falling, but by the temperature in the car and by the absence of any sound, he was able to judge that it was the deep middle of the night. The train would still be a long way from Minsk, a long way even from the border, so he supposed that it must have stopped at a signal and that in a few minutes it would get going again.

Somehow, the immobilisation of the train made the cold inside the freight car more intense and the ghost of breath that filled the space around and above Hector became agitated and began a strange kind of wailing.

The train moved. But it was going backwards, Hector could tell by the way his body rolled. And then it stopped again. Hector raised his head off his knapsack, to hear better, to see better, but he could hear and see nothing except the ghost in the air.

What Hector couldn't know was that the train had been rerouted into a siding because the line further east was temporarily closed by snow. What he couldn't know either was that the driver of the second freight had forgotten all about him and, once the train was safe in its siding, got down from his cab and walked away across the white fields towards a village, in search of a warm fire and a bed for the rest of the night. So Hector lay there, waiting for the train to resume its journey, while the soft snow piled up on the roof of the box car.

After an hour had passed, he tried to move himself towards the edge of the car, so that he could bang on the doors with his feet, but he found that his body was unwilling to move. It asked him to let it rest. He attempted, then, to call out. He knew that a human voice inside a freight train would probably make the kind of sound that disturbed one's peace and altered nothing in the world, but he tried to call nevertheless. 'Train driver!' he said. 'Help me!' It was a whisper, not a shout. Hector believed that he was shouting, but he was only murmuring. And anyway, the driver of the second freight was a mile away.

He was sitting by a fire with a schoolteacher and his wife, drinking vodka and eating poppyseed cakes.

After his efforts at calling, Hector's throat felt sore and he was afflicted suddenly by a desperate, unbearable thirst. He had no memory of where his water bottle was or when he had last seen it, but what he did remember was the solitary lemon he had put into his knapsack on the morning of his departure. And his longing, now, to suck the juice from this lemon became so great that he succeeded in extracting one hand from the blanket and with this one hand reached behind his head to try to undo the fastenings of his knapsack.

He could picture with absolute precision the colour, shape and texture of the lemon, as clearly as he could picture the icy Russian lake and the grey dacha beside it, in which he and his beloved sister would live. And his yearning for the freshness of the juice of the lemon was so deep, so absolute, that into his search for the precious fruit he put every last ounce of his strength.

The snow stopped falling an hour before sunrise and the sky cleared and the dawn was bright.

Woken by the winter sunlight, the driver of the freight to Minsk remembered at this instant the German soldier he'd agreed to hide in one of his box cars in return for DM5.

He dressed hurriedly, tugging on his overcoat and his hat, and let himself out of the schoolteacher's house.

The snow was thick on the fields. The man wasn't young. Trying to make his way through this deep snow was exhausting for him and it took him the best part of half an hour to reach the train.

He opened the door of Hector's box car and stared in. The light on the snow had blinded him and, for a moment, he could see nothing. 'Hello!' he called. 'Hello! It is morning.'

Hector was lying face up, one arm behind his head that rested on his knapsack. The German face had the pallor of bone, but there was a smile on it, as if, in his last moments Hector had glimpsed something strangely beautiful.

The train driver walked a few paces from the car and fumbled to light a cigarette.

He stood in the snow, thinking.

It didn't take him long to decide what he was going to do. He was going to leave Hector exactly where he was. He wasn't even going to touch him or cover his face. Even if the day remained fine, the cold in the box car would preserve his body and, with a bit of luck, the train would get to Minsk before nightfall.

At the depot, the freight would be unloaded by rail workers from Belarus, and so it would be they who would find the stowaway. In this way, provided he remembered to get rid of the German currency, the driver would have shifted the burden of responsibility. The dead German, wearing some kind of military uniform, would become a Russian problem.

Marina Lewycka

A HARD-LUCK STORY

Everybody has a hard-luck story. Take this woman that shows up at the deportation centre I work at, quite nice looking, dark skin, big brown eyes, with two kids, one is just a baby. She's booked in for a deportation flight back to wherever she come from. Somewhere I've never heard of.

'You're going home,' I tell her.

She starts crying. She says she wants to stay.

'Pliss. Pliss help me. You no understand.'

Anyway, she knows a bit of English, once you get used to her funny accent, and while we're sat waiting for the flight to take her home, she won't stop talking. She was a doctor back home, she tells me, and her husband was a professor. Well, anybody can say that, can't they? Her husband was in some kind of political opposition group in their country and he was arrested after a student demonstration in the university. She claims that put her and her kids in danger.

'It's always been my belief that you should keep out of politics,' I tell her. 'Politics never does any good.'

Then her hubby disappeared. She says he was killed. I say, you can't prove it, can you? You've got to have proof, otherwise you could be making it up, couldn't you? Everybody that comes here has a hard-luck story.

She tells me that a cousin that worked for the government warned her she was on the danger list. She was scared so she did a runner.

'Whoa, hang on, lady,' I say. 'Just because your hubby disappears, it doesn't mean you're in danger. I mean, he could of gone off with another woman.'

I'm just joking, like, but she doesn't even smile. She's the serious type. Too serious for me.

Well, she says she had a bit of money saved up, and she used it to get as far as Libya in a truck with her kids. They had to hide under a tarpaulin surrounded by chickens. Must have been a cluckin' good ride, I say, but she doesn't laugh. No sense of humour. You've got to have a sense of humour in this world, haven't you?

When they reached the port where they were going to get the boat over the Med, loads of people were there, swarms of them. All heading for England, you can be sure. It's because of our benefit system, it just encourages them. 'Me, I'm a taxpayer. I've got my own family to look after, and they don't pay us security guards much.' I say, 'It's bloody hard work, trying to keep you lot under control. You don't get no thanks from nobody. So don't expect no sympathy from me.'

Then the men driving the truck took the rest of her money off of her. She didn't have anything left to pay the captain to get on the boat. So the captain said he would give her a ride if she slept with him. Well, I'm not going to pass judgement on that. You've got to be broadminded in this world, haven't you? If that's what it took, I says, good luck to him.

They had to wait for a couple of days, because the sea was rough. Then they got the OK to board. She can't say for sure how many was on the boat, but waving her arms about she explains it was no bigger than the room we're in, and there must have been at least a hundred people, kids, babies and all, packed on top of each other like sardines in a tin. Nobody could move. Soon it was pitch dark, and they were out in the middle of the sea, swaying from side to side.

You could hear the creaking of the boat, sounds of people throwing up, kids crying, and the tuk tuk tuk of the engine. She makes a noise like an outboard motor. The woman next to her had a little baby that wouldn't stop whining. All they had was plastic bottles of water. No food. Well, that would just make them throw up more, wouldn't it? Then it went quiet. The tuk tuk tuk of the engine had stopped. They heard men's voices and splashing out at sea. Everyone that could move went over to one side to see what was going on. They started to shout. In the moonlight, it looked like the captain and the other two men crewing the boat had bailed out into a little inflatable dinghy and they'd took the motor. Off it went back toward the lights of land. Tuk tuk tuk.

All night they drifted, and when daylight came, there was no land in sight, only the sea, in whatever direction you looked. The wind had come up, the sky was grey, and the sea had got more choppy. By now everyone had finished their water. Someone give his last few drops to the woman with the baby, which was sucking on her tit now, fast asleep. As the sun come up, the waves went down, it got hotter, and people started to take their coats off. Maybe that's what helped to save them. Then somebody spotted land – at first it looked just like a grey smudge on the horizon, and they were drifting towards it. But as everyone shifted over to that side of the boat, a big wave came and slapped them on the other side. The boat turned over. Everybody was tipped in the sea, splashing and floundering around, trying to find something floating to grab onto. She managed to grab onto an empty plastic water-container and with her other hand she hung onto her little girl, but she couldn't see her boy. She feared he was among them trapped under the upturned boat. He never came up.

At that moment somebody spotted a motor-boat speeding towards them from the direction of the land. They waved and shouted for help, and the people on the motor-boat threw down some lifebuoys and pulled them up out of the water. Then she saw something that looked like a little bundle bobbing about on the water nearby. It was the baby, floating face up on the waves, thrashing about with its arms and legs, yelling its little head off. She grabbed hold of it, and took it with her on the motor-boat. When they got to the island, they had to jump back in the water, because the motor-boat turned back to go and help the others still in the sea. But there were people on the shore waiting to help them, who waded into the water, reaching out their hands. Smiling like angels.

As she said that she started to cry again.

'This is the first time anyone is good to us. We feel safety.'

Some people couldn't be saved, like her son, and the baby's mother, who had been trapped underneath the boat. The bodies were washed up next day on the beach, but she never found her son. She walked up and down the beach crying his name. She makes a noise like a cow mooing. I looks at her. She's crying, and shaking. It must be quite hard, losing your kid like that.

'Never mind,' I say. 'You'll soon be back home.'

They had to stay outside in a square while they waited for official checks and all that. The Angels, as she called them, Do-gooders I call them, brought food and water, and blankets when night came. They brought her a bottle of milk for the baby. She still had the dead woman's baby. Nobody knew it wasn't hers.

'But what made you come to England?' I say. I mean she could have gone anywhere in Europe. The Germans are welcoming thousands of them, mad buggers.

'In school I learn English. I learn England is good country.'

'Not any more it in't. Too many foreigners.'

A man that was hanging around the camp said he could get her to England in the back of a lorry. All she had left to pay him was her gold earrings. They had stones in them, jewels she said, so she give them to him. Two rubies. She had to sleep with him too, and one of his mates.

The way she described it, it wasn't exactly a luxury ride in the back of the truck. They were in a compartment at the back, behind the boxes of dried fruit, crowded in with twenty other people, suffocating and dark. They didn't see daylight for four days. They only let them off at night to go to the toilet. That's when the driver raped her, and one of the other women. Her face twisted up as she said it.

'He'd never get away with that around here, love. We've got rules,' I say.

They gave them water to drink, and some bread. That was all. She thinks they went on another boat. She could feel the rolling and swaying movement and she was terrified in case they were pitched into the sea again, still locked in their compartment. She thought they would never get out alive.

'That must of been the ferry over the Channel. Safe as houses,' I say.

Then they felt the vibration of the lorry engine and the bump of the wheels on the road. They were driving again. After some time the truck suddenly stopped, and the door opened. They were on a narrow road in between some fields in the middle of nowhere. It was night time. 'Get out!' said the men driving the truck, and started pulling them out of the back. 'Quick! Quick! You are in England!' Then the truck drove off and left them there. They started to walk down the road. It was dark and cold. It was raining.

'That's England all right,' I says.

There were a few lights of houses set back from the road, but nobody was about. A car passed them, with its headlights blazing, and they waved, but it didn't stop. Apart from that they didn't see a soul. Then someone shouted out, 'Police!' A police car come down the road, and they all started to run, scattering into the fields. Someone must have spotted them and called the cops.

But she didn't run. She was too tired. And she'd heard that in England the police don't arrest you for no reason. They're there to help you. Sometimes you wonder how stupid people can be. Serves them right, really.

That's how she ended up in this place, waiting to be deported back to wherever she come from. Then I hear another sound. It's the sound of her aircraft approaching.

'Pliss! Pliss!' she moans.

'Look,' I says, 'it's not up to me, lady, I'm just a security guard. You're an economic migrant, not a refugee. For all we know, your hubby is waiting to come and join you as soon as you've got your paperwork sorted.'

'Pliss! Pliss!' She wraps her arms around me and tries to kiss me. I won't pretend I'm not tempted. Like I said, she's quite nice looking. One or two of the guards at the Centre do take advantage of the female residents that way, making all sorts of promises they know they can't keep. In my opinion, that's cruel. I'm not like that.

'I'm sorry, love, there's nothing I can do. It's too late now. Even if I let you run off, they'll catch you before you get to the fence. And I've got my own problems. See, I've only been at this Centre four months. Before that, I was unemployed for over a year. I got depression. Then I had my benefit docked because I missed an appointment at the Job Centre. I had to go on the food bank. So I was lucky to get this job, and I can't afford any funny business.'

She's not listening. She just stares out of the window, watching the plane land. Big tears are rolling down her face, and I do feel a bit sorry for her, but what can you do? As it taxis towards us, she jumps up and starts rattling and banging on the door, but of course it's locked, and all the furniture here is bolted down. We're used to these scenes. People often get emotional at this stage.

Then the supervisor comes in with her black bag, and she's got the sedative ready, and I grab the woman's arm and hold it out for her. Just a little prick and no more trouble from you, lady. She slides down onto the floor, and I give the baby to the little girl to hold, so she stops crying and starts rocking it.

'That's a nice touch, Colin,' says the supervisor. 'Keep things calm and steady. It's better for everybody if they go quietly. Makes it easier for us and for them.'

She's nice, our supervisor.

Then after the plane's took off she comes up to me and says in that same steady voice, 'I've got some bad news for you, Colin. Our firm has lost the contract for this centre. Somebody made a complaint, one of the do-gooders that come around poking their noses in. Apparently, one of our staff assaulted a female resident. Ssh! Don't say it!' She puts a finger on her lips. 'I know you're not like that. I know it's not fair, everybody has to suffer because of one bad apple, but what can you do? So we're going to have to let some of the staff go. It's last in, first out. That's the rule. Sorry about that. If you want to call in at the office next week, I'll check to see if we've got any other vacancies coming up.'

Like I said, everybody has a hard-luck story.

Nick Barlay
AN ACCIDENTAL COUNTRY

My mother recently said, for the first time, that it's criminal to force people out of their country. Almost sixty years ago, that's exactly what happened to her and my father. They had married in September 1956, just before the Hungarian Revolution erupted the following month. What precipitated their decision to flee was not simply the general desire of Hungarians to avoid impending Soviet tyranny or the fact that my father would have faced arrest for political reasons. Specifically, it was the Soviet tank shell that, in early November, came through the toilet window and blew up their flat.

My parents were among the estimated 200,000 Hungarians, average age twenty-five, who fled the murderous Soviet invasion, leaving behind siblings, parents and grandparents. Years later, when my father reestablished contact with friends who had stayed behind, they told him how they would sit in their old haunts, mistaking every other face for a disappeared friend or relative. Those who left found it hard to shake off their memories, their emotional ties, their homesickness. Those who stayed saw ghosts.

To this day, a pair of Hungarian verbs defines a nation: *menni,* to go, and *maradni,* to stay. In the sense of these verbs, there was a revolution in every family. It confronted each family's cohesion, and often tore it apart. On the tenth anniversary of the Revolution, the émigré writer Arthur Koestler noted that Hungarians had been 'strewn all over the world' as if by a 'centrifugal force'. Centrifugal forces work in mysterious ways, sticking people flat, spinning people around, throwing people far and wide. For those that are thrown, every country becomes an accidental country, a waiting room not a terminus.

Without a doubt, the Revolution of 1956 is a reflecting pool in which people have always seen what they wanted to see. In Hungary, there's a book for every bullet hole, and there are lots of bullet holes. But those who flee bullets have only one thing on their minds: how to cross the first border they come to. Nothing is reflected; everything is projected. The empty future counts, not the past with its tangled roots, its overgrown graves, its complex genealogies, its heirlooms and sentimental souvenirs, its friendships, and of course its mortal threats.

The vast majority of Hungarian refugees, those that were not shot or arrested or cheated by opportunistic 'guides', did cross a border, the one to Austria. In 1956, there was little choice. Yugoslavia, Romania or Czechoslovakia were geographical options but the only realistic destination was Austria. It represented the door to the West, to peace and to freedom. As the old joke goes: a Hungarian tries to escape to Austria but is caught and given a short prison sentence. On his release, he immediately tries to escape again to Austria. He is caught and given a short prison sentence. On his release, he tries to escape a third time, this time to the Soviet Union. He is caught and given life in a lunatic asylum.

Browse the newspapers: change the names of the countries; fill in as appropriate. The truth is that refugees don't know where they will end up but they do know where they cannot end up. For the Hungarian refugees in Vienna, any country beyond the Iron Curtain, and with no direct ties to it, would do. So they visited the embassies to see which country would take them. My parents registered with the German police and with the Intergovernmental Committee for European Migration. They went to the American Joint Distribution Committee and the Catholic Relief Services. Since nobody could decide how to classify them, they received a variety of papers, as refugees, *Flüchtling*, as those seeking the right of asylum, *Asylrecht*, and as *Auswanderer*, emigrants. They could have ended up in Australia or Argentina. Only an accident brought them to Britain: an empty bus that had brought clothes donated by British students was filled with refugees for the return trip by a sympathetic British consul.

One day, many years later, each of my parents filled in a complex form. It was the 'Application by an Alien for a Certificate of Naturalisation'. The aliens had to be over twenty-one years old 'and not of unsound mind'. They had to be 'of good character'. They had to have 'sufficient knowledge of the English language'. They had to advertise their intentions in two local papers. And, within one month of the certificate being granted, they had to swear an oath of allegiance: 'I swear by Almighty God that I will be faithful and bear true allegiance to Her Majesty, Queen Elizabeth the Second, Her Heirs and Successors, according to Law.' On 18 January 1963, the applicants, 'Istvan Bokor also known as Stephen Barlay and formerly Istvan Berger', and his wife, Agota or Agatha Bokor, also known as Barlay, became citizens of the United Kingdom.

Naturalisation documents are the final destination of all previous documents. All paperwork flows that way or it flies that way or it is carried, smuggled and dispatched that way. Naturalisation represents the possible end to the question of identities. It's when an accidental country becomes home.

My parents never hesitated to call Britain home. Having survived the Holocaust only to have to escape a second totalitarianism, they ended up, via a refugee camp, in London. There, they merged with other immigrants of the 1950s, rooming with post-Windrush Jamaicans in the squalid suburbs of the capital. They were no longer in transit, no longer seeking a place.

There's a short, personal, experimental film made in 1958 by the Hungarian refugee Robert Vas, who would commit suicide in 1978. *Refuge England* begins with a refugee's disorienting arrival and his search for an address. It ends with a set dinner table in a place the refugee can call home. But the difference between 'home' and 'a home' is like the difference between 'identity' and 'an identity'. Finding refuge in a country is one thing. Who to be in that country is another. The names my parents trailed behind them stretched far back in history. Even if successful refugees, the ones who make it, can look back on their experience as an adventure, a part of them never leaves their country of origin.

That year, 1956, posed three big questions, existential questions that transcend time: whether to stay or to go; where to go; and, once you had got there, who to be. But the questions posed in such a year, at such an irreversible moment, remain unanswered, year after year, decade after decade. Life is lived in relation to that year. Every refugee has such a year, one that snags, one that only seems to elapse, as if it had reached a temporal border without ever managing to cross it completely. It's a year that glitches, that resolutely resists change, that lasts forever.

And all of this is the case for one reason: the crime that caused it is rarely, if ever, redressed. Great crimes cast great shadows, and it's always ordinary people who live in those shadows, eternal refugees who belong neither here nor there, who can only hope for a home from home. Now, as then, Britain and many other countries, including Hungary itself, are facing one of the greatest ever trans-national movements of people.

Ironically, and poignantly, it was not simply that fleeing Hungarians were granted refuge in 1956 by many other countries. Thirty-three years later, in 1989, the Hungarian border is where the Iron Curtain began to crumble, not at the Berlin Wall as is often supposed. It was Hungarian border guards, in the summer of that year, who allowed in tens of thousands of refugees from Romania and, shortly afterwards, decided not to prevent East German tourists who were 'holidaying' in Hungary from crossing into Austria. The question that accompanies such movements of people is constant, and simple. As my mother put it: how can you force a person who has been forced out of their country back in?

A year ago, my mother suffered an aneurysm, akin to a stroke. Among other things, it affected her short-term memory. By contrast, her long-term memory remains intact. She has lost track of time but not of history. When she watches the news, with its families of ordinary people waiting at ordinary borders, she thinks of Hungary six decades ago. While she and my father lived happily in their accidental country, they did not forget the crime that forced them there. More importantly, they would not deny others the same happy accident.

Ruth Padel

Excerpts from

CHILDREN OF STORM

IMMIGRATION COUNTER AND THE GATES OF IVORY

They're back to Canada after summer in Mumbai.
'Think they're still awake now, Grandpa
and Granny?'
Wails fill the cabin as lights go down on our long
haul flight
and we're in the Moonlight World of the
Small Mammal
House at the Zoo. Her face is a fire-lit mask
as she settles their blankets and the rest of us try
looking this night in its indigo eye, pleated
like inner petals of a gentian. We doze
while in the Mumbai suburb where, let's suppose,
she grew up, her parents still flick through
the photos.
Home was festivals, the kitchen, the shrine of a
front room.
But that's over now, with the grandchildren abroad.

Light glimmers through the thicket of the aisle.
Roll on seven hours, and we're in Passport Control
with a flight from Abuja. The family in transit
from Mumbai have papers new-minted as snow
but here's an old guy from Nigeria, alone
with a small string bag. Behind the officer
in blue, turning every page of my passport,
a wall kiosk of Travelex
World Wide Money glows
like Santa's Magic Cave. Then I'm through,
the Mumbai lot too, but for the old man
she's called a colleague. They winnow
his papers like a rice harvest. No Travelex for him.
A man may dream his wife returns, or he returns
to her, but dreams are shadow-customers. They flit
from the underworld through two doors – one horn,
the other ivory. If his dreams have picked
the ivory, his ancestors are amusing themselves
floating illusion upward to the living.
Dreams that arrive through horn come true
but how do you know? At the Styx
of the UK Border, a gentian blossom
is forcibly removed. We progress to Luggage Claim.
Indigo petals fade, curl and close on nothing.

THE APPLE ORCHARD IN *GHOSTS*

That moment in the film
when there's no more work in the fields

and the leather-collared bull-man
gangmaster shifts them to an orchard

harvesting its last fruit
before all the Worcester Pearmains

and Red Falstaffs are torn up for ever.
Suddenly it's the 'People Will Say We're in Love' scene,

all trees, wicker baskets and sunlight
from *Oklahoma*.

England is no longer grey mud
beyond the greasy windows of the minibus

but green – yes, and real people,
gentle and sad themselves,

in a misty kitchen
offering what passes for tea.

THE PRAYER LABYRINTH

She went looking for her daughter. How many
visit Hades and live? Your only hope
is the long labyrinth of Visa Application
interviews with a volunteer from a charity
but you're not allowed to meet her.
You've been caught: by a knock on the door
at dawn, or hiding in a truck of toilet tissue
or just getting stuck in a turnstile.

You're on Dead Island: the Detention Centre.
The Russian refugees who leaped from the
fifteenth floor
of a Glasgow tower block to the Red Road
Springburn – Serge, Tatiana and their son
who, when the Immigration officers
were at the door, tied themselves together
before they jumped – knew what was coming.

Anyway you're here. Evidence of cigarette
burns all over your body has been dismissed
by the latest technology. You're dragged
from your room, denied medication
or a voice. You can't see your children,
they're behind bars somewhere else.
You go on hunger strike. You're locked
in a corridor for three days without water

then handcuffed through the biopsy
on your right breast. You've no choice
but to pray; and to walk the never-ending path
of meditation on ***not yet***. Your nightmare
was home-grown; you're seeking sanctuary.
They say you don't belong. They give you
a broken finger, a punctured lung.

PURPLE INK

She has waited three years for this. Too ashamed
to even half-tell the young woman in spectacles
tapping a purple biro on a desk

exactly what the soldiers did to her, each versatile
in his turn, she gets wrong *Date your Mother was Born,*
sees a stamp the colour of desert night descend on
her file.

CARPET KARAOKE

New life-forms are entering the world:
government agencies, like young dragons
on a moonlit beach, in a transitional period
of operation. Let's imagine you're standing
at Gatwick Airport in the Year of Our Lord
2008, and a Secretary is launching the UK
Border Agency, to be a shadow to the Home Office.

Now let's suppose you slip out of the House
of Lords onto Cornish granite, and hammer
on the Great West Door of Westminster Abbey,
yearning to sing the Office of Compline.
Rays stream in through Gothic stone, lighting up
the eleven-circuit labyrinth embedded in the floor,
and the filigree rosette at its heart
signifying compassion and enlightenment

while shadows multiply under home floorboards
and Securicor blends with G4S
whose motto is *Securing Your World* –
yes, the escort agency, silent as the Chinese word
for secrecy, where a criminal record for assault
is no barrier as security escort; providing solutions
to the problem of not enough world to go round

in the shape of escorts trained in pain compliance
who have taken a shine to one particular technique
and compare notes on it in Facebook. Ride the 24
to the end of the line, studying case histories
from the Medical Justice Network, and you find
the word 'breathing' twined through them all
like flowers through a kelim.
They hand-and-leg-cuff their deportee,

double him up on the seat, three or four
to one, and push his head between his legs.
Think iron grinding ice, think don't-want-to-look.
'They fist-squeezed his testicles, kicked
in his ribs and his stomach.' He cried, they say,
they always say, for help. But fighting for breath
he can only shout at the floor.

Courttia Newland

THE ROAD TO SILVERTOWN

The day they said we belonged to nothing and no one but ourselves, I was changing the youngest's nappy and barely heard. He lay on the sofa, eyes on the ceiling in ritual expectation, kicking drumstick legs, waiting for me to finish. I was extracting cold wipes from the pack almost without thinking, exchanging the old nappy for new, and I would like to say I was immune to the smell but of course that was impossible, I just pretended it wasn't there. Once it was a tight, sodden parcel, I threw the nappy towards the rubbish bin, watching it bounce and settle only to notice a small pile of others in the same place. It caught me for a second as I'd forgotten they were there. That's when I saw the television.

There were armoured vans like vehicles of war, men who had the dress and weaponry of soldiers but were not. There were pronouncements of politicians for and against, but the fors were in power and given the most airtime, so their voices rang loudest. I saw newscasters, excited, anxious, although it's fair to say that those in the studio were afraid. I felt the urge to stand, and did, while my youngest rolled from the sofa to play with his Lego toys. Something in their tone made me step out into the back yard. The silence of that tiny square of concrete was a balm and I swayed with the breeze, the swinging white length of clothesline, and the consoling *shush* of my neighbour's trees, thanking God my wife was more vigilant than I.

She came back with our eldest son, almost in tears. The vans had arrived just after she did, accosting people at the gates. If she hadn't got there early to find our eldest with his teacher, they both might have been herded into the vehicles. She almost pulled his arm from its socket trying to shepherd him to the bus stop, she told me, fumbling her house keys, dropping them, picking them up and walking fast even as the vans turned the corner, rumbling and slow. The last thing she saw when she looked back was the black uniformed men gathering around the teacher, pushing her towards the van, her protests. I didn't know how to respond. It seemed they wanted everyone. I listened to my wife, cursing myself for not doing so sooner.

We must leave, she told me, the detention centres were foul places our children should never see. Work colleagues had told her of coastal towns where hired boats could take us across the Channel, if things come to the worst. We had money, maybe not enough, but it was better than waiting. We avoided our eldest's tears and the haunted face of our youngest, hurrying to the bedroom where twin rucksacks bulged like muscles. We lifted them onto our backs, filling our pockets with the remnants of home. We grasped a child each by the hand and left.

The streets, taut silence. Barely any people, as the warnings were to stay home, but of course we couldn't. The thin wind, making our eyes water, our cheeks sore. The children's whimpers, their questions. Dark had come. We were grateful for its assistance, wary of its threat. An odd smell invaded the air, powdery and dense. We had no idea where to go, we just had to leave the city, so we craned our necks for signs we'd never paid attention to before. All the way we thought we'd see the vans. Our hearts pumped when cars passed, but no vans came, mostly there was only the sound of our footsteps echoing from brick walls.

On the main road, more people. Many walked as we did, bent crooked under rucksacks. Some pulled suitcases, or guided them by their side like the blind. My wife tutted, predicting those most likely to be lost. I told her to lower her voice. A few put their belongings in buggies, others had supermarket trolleys. My wife shook her head, and I nudged her. Most trailed children. The air grew moist and warm. I hadn't expected so many people to be that afraid. I clutched my rucksack strap tighter, pulling my youngest close. A small girl, a curled halo around her face, no more than six, waved a similarly dark-haired doll like a windscreen wiper. My wife gave a half smile, nodding once. The little girl, perhaps noting her seriousness, stopped waving. Her family moved fast and she disappeared into the growing landscape of shadows.

We followed in their direction. No idea where we were going, just walking. The pavement became knotted with people. My eldest bumped into a group of men, a father and his two sons in their early twenties, the father delirious and slack jawed, his sons' eyes bright in the gloom. When my eldest apologised, one of the young men, the more streetwise, lent him his corduroy baseball cap and said it was cool. My wife smiled and asked where they were headed. The streetwise one said Syria. We laughed. The younger, more nervous and straight-faced, told us boats were departing from Silvertown taking people down the estuary and over the Channel. We discussed the cost, which was reasonable. It would be better for the kids than heading to Eastbourne, the streetwise one said. A nightmare journey, he wouldn't risk it. My youngest asked how far it was to Syria. I told him a long way.

We slowed to match their pace, as the father wasn't as fast as his sons, and our children preferred not to be dragged.

We talked about what we had done, what we would do. The streetwise brother worked as a security guard in the law courts, so he and my wife had an affinity. They exchanged stories about the deportation cases they saw go to trial, the effect of laws ushered through parliament on the common people. My wife's knowledge was rudimentary; she only sat outside her employer's offices, receiving clients, but she understood enough for awareness far beyond mine and the father's, a house-husband and sufferer of poor mental health respectively. The youngest son worked in IT. He too remained silent. We exchanged food – small packets of nuts, health bars, apples and tangerines. The knot of people drew tighter, the hum of voices rising, the wind less penetrating.

I'll never forget the night. The feel of my wife's shoulder against mine. Her silence, her harsh, shallow breath. My youngest's sticky palm, the webbed flesh between our fingers. The off-beat patter of shoes meeting tarmac, a spectral drift of cigarette smoke. A far-off bark. The single emotionless eye of the moon. A peach-tinted sky, starless or so it seemed. The humming ebb of voices. Sweat making my eyes sting. I wiped them with the hand that clasped my youngest's, bending so I wouldn't have to let go. His earnest, wide brown eyes, steady on the road ahead. I tried to control my breathing, to slow it down.

We walked until fatigue burned my legs, and I was forced to lift my son into my tired arms. As far as I could see, a shambling trail of people, front and behind. Headscarves, hoodies, turbans, tracksuits, kaftans, baseball caps, long black jackets. Piercing car horns, startling my youngest. Heads leant from open windows, shouting. My wife's gasp, hands covering my eldest's ears until he fought her, pushed them away, shouting back. The streetwise brother swivelled on the spot, watching the cars disappear, fists clenched by his sides. The nervous brother kept walking, one hand on the old man's shoulder. His father's neck was bent, watching sandals and grey socks, head bobbing. We walked until the road was silent. No cars or buses, just an empty patchwork of fresh and greying tarmac, a thick black groove where buses ran, a static wave. I wanted to leave the main road, but the others said it was pointless. The road to Silvertown was straight; we'd only make it longer. I thought this unwise, but I saw their point. Half a mile further, the streetlights clicked off.

Complete darkness. Exhaled gasps, rippling murmurs. My wife's shoulder pushing harder into mine. Tiny fingers tightening. It was difficult to see. I turned towards the opposite pavement for light, but every shop window on that side was dark. Then somehow the road ahead grew bright, there was light in front and behind us, and I knew what was happening, so I pulled my wife by the shoulder, telling her to run. I dropped the rucksack, picked up my youngest and swung him onto my back as best as I could. People screamed and bumped into us, pushing where we did not want to go. The lights were blinding. I held my wife and pulled at her, sprinting without direction, I could have been going back for all I knew. I heard my youngest wailing, and felt good, God forgive me, because I knew he was with me and as long as that was true, all was well. I heard the painful cry of tyres, mute blows, shouts, I breathed in exhaust fumes and burnt rubber, felt spasms in my legs and the muscles of my arms, and all I could do was run, pulling at my wife, listening to her beg me to stop, leave her alone, but I would not, we were together, nothing was more important than that.

I wrenched at her and ran. I closed my eyes, shutting everything out for I don't know how long. She fought me, punching all over my body, trying to free herself. I admit I lost my temper, God forgive me, securing my grip by wrapping an arm around her neck and dragging her down the road that way, my youngest's arms squeezing hard, almost choking me, but I didn't let go. I kept trying to run, stumbling. The noise behind us faded and ceased. I heard the lonely, pained cry of an unseen fox. The soft glow of streetlights fell on us. I saw a dark front garden walled on all sides by a tall, flat hedge. I kicked the gate open, threw her inside roaring with pain, feeling the strain in my back and neck. Pausing to make sure no one had seen us, I followed after her. There were huge bins, one lid green, the other orange; squat, hulking guards. It was a terrible hiding place, yes, but I crouched down behind them, panting hard, lungs aching, whispering curses at my family to stop them crying so loud.

It took time to get used to the light. I was so focused on berating my youngest – telling him what they would do if we were forced into those vans, how they would arrest, beat and separate us, how we would be taken to those centres and onto the planes in cuffs if we were lucky, trying everything I could to stop his crying fit – only the little girl caught my attention. She huddled in the darkest corner of the garden, metres from the red wooden gate, the mother clutching her tight like a pillow, face damp, red, eyes puffed. The girl was tiny, shivering, blonde curls beneath a dark hood. White knee socks and dark shoes. The mother was thin, also blonde and scared, I could see that; fearful, wondering what I might do. I tried to speak with them, but the mother began wailing again, growing hysterical and I saw what my youngest had. I stood, reaching out a hand to reassure them, but the woman kicked her legs, moving herself and the child towards the shadow of the house. There was no way to rectify it. We would be caught if we stayed. I hugged my child to me and left the garden, the woman and her daughter. With the last of my strength I lifted him back onto my shoulders.

The road was bare, the houses dark, but that could only last so long. They would come, I kept telling myself. They would come. The weight of my youngest caused sweat to blind me. The streetlights twinkled into stars.

I swung him from my shoulders so we could walk, perhaps look normal. Our food was gone, as were our clothes; they were all in the rucksacks. He was sniffling, cold, complaining of hunger and I had nothing. I searched for houses with dark windows, trying their gates. Most were unsuitable. The best I found was a broad, three-storey semi-detached, all white, with a side door that perhaps led to a small alley, which might lead to a back garden. That would do. I thumbed the latch, careful as a thief. We went halfway down the alley and crouched in the dark, backs to the wall, knees up. I took my jacket off and wrapped it around him, cradling his shivering body. Of course, he couldn't sleep; he cried for most of the night. Eventually tiredness wore him out and he collapsed against me. I fought too, but after some hours my eyes closed against my will.

Warmth. Soft, soothing. I opened my eyes to morning light, shifting to allow blood into my arms and feet. My limbs prickled like the sparklers I'd lit for my youngest on Guy Fawkes; he fell beneath my armpit, snoring. I saw the night again, and tried to stop myself crying as I didn't want to wake him, but nothing could stop it, no rational thought, no hope, not even my fears. I had to let it go, or risk him seeing later. Even then, I had to force myself to be quiet in case I was heard by those who were not our friends. I wondered how long I'd been holding my breath, keeping myself inside myself, unable to empty my lungs, limbs stiff, back straight.

I let him sleep for twenty more minutes, shook him. That took another eight. The light grew and I became frantic. I stood him up before he was ready, and he almost fell against the wall. Eyes half closed, he said he was hungry. I promised we would eat as soon as we got there. He swayed as if already on the boat. That made me smile. Come, I said, hugging him to me, come. We walked from the alley, through the front garden, onto the street. It was empty. Our feet slipped in condensation. The birds conversed above our heads. A low growl of engines came from streets away. We had no choice but to walk in that direction. With luck, if we were caught, we might be reunited with his mother, my son. I pulled his hood up and took a bobbled knitted hat from my jacket, pulling it down just over my eyes. We walked between the walls of houses on either side, hand in hand. A pretty street, full of pinks, blues and yellows. I would have liked to live there one day.

The road, we discovered, was the A112. Signs and white arrows pointed towards Silvertown. Cars and heavy trucks sped by, ignoring us. Look at that, I said to my youngest, pointing up. That's good. That's good.

When I was a young boy, about his age, we lived by the sea. I'd wake in the mornings before my parents and sneak from the unlocked house to run down the incline of beach, sand falling around my heels, rushing into low tide. The sky was a canvas of shadows. Birds wandered, stiff-legged, pecking at seawater. I'd kick out, trying to splash them, lick the salt from my lips, or dig up crab holes, or sit on the sand letting the tide cool my toes. My parents scolded me when they realised where I was, and for a while that didn't deter me, but eventually they locked the front door and hid the key. We moved inland, to the city, and when I returned as a young man, a few years before I left the country for good, it was to find crumbling walls, exposed foundations, the sea eating at the place I'd once called home. I wanted to cry then too, but I could only feel the burn in my eyes, the weight in my chest, the inexplicable scratch in my throat. I stood on the path that once led to my front door, gentle water lapping my bare feet, trying to recall past times.

Katharine Quarmby
BECOMING ENGLISH

Somewhere at the back of a cupboard there's a small, battered brown suitcase, with P. B. written on it in black ink. My children used to play with it when they were dressing up as characters in the Paddington Bear books and carry it around the house with them. But it has another resonance too: whenever I catch sight of it, I think of my mother, who says it's just a little bigger than the cardboard suitcase that she and my grandmother brought to the UK, when they arrived at Croydon Airport in 1946.

My mother's name, then, was Mara Božić, and she had lived, until that point, in a country that no longer exists, but was then called Yugoslavia. My grandmother, born Isabel Garrido, to an English mother and a Spanish father, arrived in Belgrade in the 1930s, to work as a teacher. She was in an international club one day when she received a telegram informing her that she had come into a small inheritance. A dashing Bosnian Serb, Miloika Božić, overheard her exclaiming: 'I've inherited a fortune.' He wooed her and wed her, within three days.

They lived well, for a few years before the war, mostly on my grandmother's money. My grandmother changed her name to Jelisaveta Božić, renounced her English nationality, destroyed her passport and took Yugoslavian citizenship. They took a grand apartment near the Patriarch's Palace and employed a maid, as befitted their place in society.

My grandmother recalled those days, years later, in a letter to a Serbian journalist: 'In my little drawing room I entertained – with fruit conserve, cakes and coffee – lady friends, English, Serbian and Jewish.' They bought a car with luxurious leather upholstery and employed a driver. In 1937, the year my mother was born, my mother's cousins, Mile and Yela, arrived in Belgrade from Brussels, with their widowed father, Voija. My mother was doted on; she grew up learning to play the grand piano and dance ballet. In the summer they took trips to the remote family dacha, entwined in creepers, in Bosnia. My mother recalled, recently, one trip there, when she was a shade less than four years old, seeing the villagers perform an ancient fertility rite: 'The whole village was out in the fields. They carried long poles on which bundles hung, which they lit and waved over the fields.'

Then came the war. In 1941, after a coup d'état, the Germans invaded. Life was tolerable at first, my grandmother recalled, as the troops were disciplined. My mother even danced a solo from the Nutcracker Suite at the National Ballet in front of an audience that included German officers. The family travelled to the dacha once more, thinking it was remote enough to be safe, and my grandmother stuffed the upright piano there with sugar and flour. But, one day, German officers came knocking on the door and entered. They gestured for someone to play the piano, and Yela sat down to play, but the piano made no noise. One of the officers lifted the lid to find my grandmother's store. On this occasion, the officers laughed, and neither took the store nor harmed the family.

But my grandmother's original nationality put the family at risk. English citizens were in grave danger of being sent to concentration camps. (Her sister, Eva, who was married to a Frenchman and was living in Paris, was also at risk. A friend forged a birth certificate for her, to say she was born in Brittany.) My grandmother spoke to my mother only in Serbo-Croat, and hoped that nobody would betray them. My mother remembers her Jewish friends from school being rounded up by the Nazis. Their mothers were put on one open cart and the children on another. They were told that they were to be taken to a place of safety and sang as they went. They were never seen again.

Food became scarce; my grandmother sold the grand piano for a pound of lard. She decided that eating horse was acceptable. When a man came to the door, selling meat with black, coarse hairs on it and she realised it was dog, however, she refused. They weren't quite that desperate. My mother can still remember the day when my grandmother bought an egg – just the one – and boiled it. My mother ate it, as her parents and the maid looked on.

The Allied Forces carpet-bombed Belgrade over the Orthodox Easter, in April 1944, with 600 planes, and the loss of over 1,000 civilian lives. The family decided to evacuate and so they walked out, one summer morning, to the small village of Rušanj, just over ten miles south from the city. My mother recalls: 'As we were walking the sirens went and the bombing started. We took shelter in a house. When we came out the house opposite had been hit. We reached the top of a hill and looked back at Belgrade. A curtain of flames hung across the whole city.' Rušanj was on a rough track and was, thankfully, largely untroubled by Allied bombing raids. A village family took them in, refusing any payment. They were not the only ones: that small village of some 2,000 people took in around 1,800 refugees, my grandmother recorded, with little fuss. (Remember those numbers, and the lack of fuss, when we pat ourselves on the back for taking in a few thousand Syrian refugees.) My mother herded pigs, barefoot, with the other children, and slept in the henhouse. By day the village women picked lice off the children, one by one, and squashed them between their fingernails. My grandmother, who had studied Classics at Cambridge University, distanced herself, purposely, from what was going on by recording, in her head, the similarities between life in the village and Homeric and Classical tales she had read. Personal horrors intruded, all the same: one day the news came that cousin Mile, a Chetnik, had been gunned down by the Nazis.

My mother and grandmother survived the war, and went back to Belgrade – liberated, if that is the right word, by the Communists. My grandmother was reluctant to send my mother back to school, but was forced to do so. At the age of eight, her class was marched, crocodile fashion, to a theatre, and shown black and white footage of the gas ovens in the concentration camps – images still seared into her memory. The teachers forced the children to chant Communist slogans. By the autumn of 1945 my grandmother was pregnant again. She had only just survived septicaemia with my mother. She wanted to come to England. But her husband refused to accompany her – and there was another problem.

They were no longer English citizens. Their English relations had to beg – and eventually pay a bond – to the Home Office. The letter they wrote to officials was, at the very least, economical with the truth. The relatives wrote that my grandmother needed an operation in the UK (no word of the pregnancy) and that she had inherited some property (which was not true). But this sentence, of course, was the clincher: 'We, the undersigned, uncle and aunt of the above... guarantee to be responsible for the maintenance of her and her child in England so no charge will fall on the State.' The application was successful and one icy day in January 1946 my mother and grandmother flew to England, over the Alps and via Paris, in a Dakota transport plane. My mother doesn't remember packing that small suitcase except for one object; my grandmother brought with her a book of Yugoslavian poetry for children, which she had illustrated with hand-painted watercolours. My mother lost her father, her mother tongue, her home and her country. But she gained a place of safety and a new homeland.

They were in that grey land between economic migrants and refugees – just as many are today, because, in truth, things are not simple and lines are not black and white and half-truths or even outright lies have to be told so people can stay safe. My grandmother fled, eventually, because she thought she might die in childbirth, her marriage had failed and she didn't want my mother to grow up under Communist rule. I suspect she would have failed any test for refugee status today. In fact, in many ways, she was that horror of tabloid horrors – a health migrant. She had endured Nazi occupation and kept my mother safe through sheer courage but that isn't enough to deserve safety, then, or now. By the time my mother was eight she had been a refugee, or internally displaced person, or economic migrant (depending on your terms), twice, and lived under the two 'great' dictatorships of the twentieth century.

My mother was sent to school, in Woking in Surrey, without a word of English, at the age of nine. She remembers standing in the playground, and hearing children 'babbling' all around her. She forgot her Serbo-Croat within three weeks and dubs the Home Secretary Theresa May's plan to send refugees back to their country of origin once it is considered 'safe' cruel in the extreme. For unaccompanied minors, who will be sent back when they are young adults, this seems particularly harsh. My mother, like other young children, lost her culture and language very fast and assimilated fast too – she had to. How else would she have survived in a playground where there were no other children from Yugoslavia? She says she would have been devastated to have lost the new life she had made by being sent back to a country she hardly knew at the age of eighteen.

My grandmother re-named her Mary, and after some months living with aunts, they moved to Cambridge. They were very poor – my grandmother had to look after a baby and raise a daughter. She taught students in the evening – and she turned their war-time experiences, about those months in Rušanj, into a book, entitled *Women in a Village*. It was successful and helped them to recover financially, after those first few years of poverty in England.

Later, my mother attended teacher-training college and, one summer, worked at the Chivers jam factory in Cambridge. She met a young Yorkshire man, a Cambridge University student. They fell in love over an assembly line of Christmas pudding trays. Later they got married, and both became teachers. They had three sons, but they wanted a girl, so decided to adopt. They didn't care what colour the baby was, my dad told the adoption society, mindful of the news of abandoned babies from Hong Kong and elsewhere. So they were offered a three-month-old 'coloured' child, in the parlance of the time, a half-Persian girl who was, at that time, 'hard to place'. (Most adoptive parents then didn't want a child of mixed racial heritage. Most ended up in children's homes.) The birth father, an Iranian sailor who desperately wanted to keep the child and take her back to Iran, was not allowed to do so. He was forced to relinquish her and they became my parents. I was very lucky. There's a twist here – later he became a political prisoner, after the Iranian Revolution, during which he experienced imprisonment, torture and mock execution. He is lucky to be alive and would almost certainly qualify for refugee status if he ever decided to leave Iran. It took me many years of searching to find him and eventually meet him, first in the UK and then to visit him, in a rather clandestine way, in Iran. His story has emerged, piecemeal, over those visits.

My mum lost her father and her homeland, but her Yugoslavian relatives did keep in touch. And what a colourful bunch they were. Her grandfather, Kosta Božić, a Serbian cleric, was accused along with a number of others at Banja Luka in 1916, in an infamous trial connected to the assassination of Archduke Franz Ferdinand. He was found guilty of high treason and was sentenced to death. His sentence was then commuted and he was released to become Dean of Sarajevo, before he succumbed to tuberculosis, in 1919. On the old oak dresser, in my parents' sitting room, sits a nutcracker, carved out of a dark wood during those years he spent in prison – the only object my mother has retained of her life in Yugoslavia, after the poetry book was lost. His sons, Voija, Ljubisha and Miloika, the latter of whom was just twelve, afraid that they would be imprisoned too, left the country at the time of his trial. They were, in effect, child refugees; they walked through Bosnia, Croatia, Slovenia, Italy, into France and finally arrived in Brussels, penniless – a journey of eight hundred miles. They must have worked and begged their way across Europe. My mother, seeing the young Syrian men on the TV, says that they always remind her of her uncles and father and the long march they took, to Brussels and a place of safety.

They started to make a new life for themselves, although Miloika went back to Belgrade as the political situation relaxed. Ljubisha stayed in Brussels and became a banker. Voija stayed there till 1937, when he returned to Belgrade with Mile and Yela as a widower. In the 1950s, under Communist rule, he forgot himself one day and swore allegiance to King Peter in front of a friend, who betrayed him to the Communists. He ended up in prison for five years – just like his father before him. Despite all these troubles the memories my mother and I have of Ljubisha, Yela and Voija are happy ones: they were joyous and generous people, with a sense of fun. Ljubisha and Yela liked a tipple – the former loved the Slav liqueur, slivovitz, and Yela the finest malt, topped with a Gauloise.

My mother's Spanish relations were no more law-abiding. Isabel's mother was English by birth, but her father, Leandro Garrido, had been a much-loved Spanish artist, and his father before him a well-known Spanish Republican MP, artist and journalist, Fernando Garrido. Fernando had many spells in and out of prison in Spain for his socialist beliefs; he would write an inflammatory article or pamphlet, annoy the government and dodge the law by going over the border to France, Portugal, and then the UK. He came to the north of England to study the co-operative movement (which he later popularised in Spain in his writings) and got to know the Chartist Thomas Allsop in the 1850s, on one of his flights as a political refugee.

Allsop looked, on first glance, like a pillar of the community. He was an English stockbroker. He had a wide circle of friends, including Samuel Taylor Coleridge, Charles Lamb, William Cobbett and Robert Owen. But instead of mellowing with age, he became involved in violent radical politics. While Fernando Garrido was in England, Allsop was involved in buying the shell casings for three bombs that were then thrown by Felice Orsini at Napoleon III in Paris on 14 January 1858. Orsini – who had taken refuge in London – had travelled to Paris on Allsop's passport, which had been issued to him by the Foreign Office. Eight bystanders died and 150 were injured. Allsop fled to New Mexico to escape arrest, returning when Palmerston's government had fallen and it was clear that he would not be prosecuted for his involvement in the plot. The Orsini plot also tested Britain's long-held policy of tolerance towards political exiles and refugees to its limits – but it held until the 1905 Aliens Act.

Allsop's daughter, Elizabeth, was a governess. Fernando Garrido had met her in Rochdale around this febrile time, and they fell in love. Their third son, Leandro, was born in 1868. He, like his father, showed a talent for art, and studied at the South Kensington School, where he made a name for himself and taught the young Augustus John among others.

Leandro is much remembered and family papers document how much he was loved. His father had died before he was sixteen, and Leandro was already showing signs of the tuberculosis that would carry him off. He spent his summers in Herne Bay, with his English cousins, one of whom, May, remembered him in a document I found among family papers. She talked about the last summer she spent with him, in the house in Herne Bay, kept by two maiden aunts – Aunt Liz, who was hospitable, and Aunt Jane, who was less so. 'It was after Aunt Liz died; the cousin who reigned in her stead didn't love the friendless and feeble, tho she kept up the house's reputation for hospitality... I know Leo must have felt on sufferance... Something had gone wrong at supper; he had grumbled... he had swung out into the paddock, leaving his supper untouched and I, I supposed, had run after him. I feel myself keeping pace with him, arm tucked under his; I know he told me of his father and "once upon a time" and I remember almost the tone and gesture "my name is Leandro Ramon di Garrido, but of course we have dropped the 'di'".'

Leandro, that proud young man who had lost not just the 'di' but so much more as his family had fled for safety across so many borders, left for Paris to teach art, and there he met my great-grandmother, Louisa Mary, and painted her, and asked her to marry him. In the portrait we have of Louisa Mary, her eyes are sparkling with love. They married in the summer of 1903 and they settled in Etaples and had two daughters, my grandmother and my great-aunt. Leandro died of tuberculosis, in Grasse, Switzerland, in 1909. He was mourned, and not just by his family.

After Leandro's untimely death, the writer Arnold Bennett wrote to my great-grandmother, 'I had a great esteem for your husband as a painter, and I have a real sympathy with your temperament.' He put himself at her disposition, 'either now or later'. A number of Leandro Garrido's paintings are still held by art galleries in the UK, due partly to the intervention of Percy Bate, the Secretary of the Royal Glasgow Institute of the Fine Arts. He wrote to my great-grandmother on 10 May 1909, of her husband's death, 'It is indeed bad for you. And the loss to the world of art is incalculable', and also placed himself at her aid. The family returned to the UK, with the girls going to boarding school and Louisa devoting herself to the Suffragist cause, although she, too, was showing signs of tuberculosis and died a few years after her husband. And so the girls became orphans in their teenage years. Isabel, my grandmother, and Eva, my great-aunt, left England as adults. They never took root here and instead both got marooned on the Continent during the Second World War.

From Allsop onwards, five generations of my mother's family on that side have had to, at moments, flee across borders to find a place of safety or economic security. Sometimes that has been because of their own actions, or those of their relations. This is true on my mother's Serbian side as well – her grandfather was imprisoned because of his undoubted sympathy with the Serbian nationalist movement, and her father and uncles fled because they feared being imprisoned because of their father's deeds or words. But my mother and grandmother were blameless – and who are we, living in safety and comfort, to make such judgements of people in fear of their lives, anyhow? Luckily, at the moment when they and other relatives needed help, there were English people who appreciated that whatever the circumstances, people in flight need shelter and reached out a hand of welcome. And, of course, some generations even took on that wonderful, shifting thing: an English identity – whatever that means.

If George Orwell is right about Englishness, in his

wonderful essay on identity, it means gentleness, distrust of authority, decency (and a love of flowers, really?). I think my mother has nailed it. She has become English. The reasons for that are, I think, two-fold: she married my father, of course, who she describes as her rock, whose identity stretches way back in this island, through generations of Yorkshire farming and Lincolnshire hunting folk; and she made friends with a girl called Rachel, from a Quaker family in Cambridge. That family took her under their wing and she became a surrogate daughter to them. They helped her take an informal but pertinent citizenship test – hearing the first ever episode of *The Archers*, in 1951. She remembers: 'That day is imprinted on my mind. We had a high tea in their kitchen. We all sat at their table – the three sisters, Rachel, Vanessa, Esther, and their parents – and then we sat round the enormous wireless to listen and right at the end the battery faded and we never heard the end.' That love affair with *The Archers* has never diminished. A year later, she walked into Cambridge Police Station, on Parkside, and was naturalised. She remembers bursting into tears of relief. She felt then that she finally was somewhere she could call home. The Home Office should consider this when they send eighteen-year-old young adults back to their 'homeland'. It was once. It almost certainly isn't any more.

My family has taken on many identities in its time – on my Yorkshire father's side, proudly that of course – while on my mother's side are all those nomadic figures, fleeing one mishap or another, economic or political, changing nationality in the process: English, Spanish and Yugoslavian, before becoming English once again. That solidity on one side and nomadism on the other made my family the perfect one to adopt me – a half-Iranian, half-English baby (and, later, to welcome my Iranian birth father when he visited too).

Some families are made, not born, through ties of love,

rather than blood – and I think this is true of nations as well, like the English and wider British identities, which are, at their best, welcoming, mixed and hospitable. The best of the English spirit is, for me, contained in that letter from our long-dead cousin May, talking about cousin Leandro, and how he should be welcomed by the maiden aunts and the house full of English cousins. Do we, today, welcome the 'friendless and the feeble' or do we make the next generation of people with nowhere to go feel awkward, unwelcome, unwanted? Does that attitude really 'become' the English? I would rather we 'kept up the house's reputation' for tolerance and hospitality.

Roma Tearne
THE COLOUR OF POMEGRANATES

Baghdad. 25 March 2003

He saw it appear out of nowhere and he began to run.

All five children were playing outside.

'God. Oh!' he shouted. 'Quick. Now. Amo. Run, run!'

The children looked up, had just enough time to hear the roar, see the flash of metal, before the missile exploded over the roof of the house.

> Darken sky forever violent run, *run* where are they I can't see
> heads or torso
> severed or ripped choices which one which way
> whose is it anyway
> he is screaming I am screaming they are screaming tossing words
> small limbs toes hands random man-sized super-sized kebab thighs
> grasping lungs gathering black dust
> arms legs another torso here a severed head
> over there
> one spinning madly not much you can do with that
> pomegranate seeds or droplets of blood wide-
> eyed and surprised can't be pomegranates the

colour's wrong
blowing out sucking in ripped off metal shutter
rattling teeth or train wheels
rocks and jolts and fires and don't touch the wires
gaping killer ends
exposed thoughts like electric cables hanging by
a fuse
splinters too
duck down scream Khalid scream where are you
buckled concrete bedroom furniture never before
views of other people's lives and where *is* he I don't
care about other people's
concrete floors shuddering into rubble and in the
corner of our eyes small things cart wheeling into a
new kind of missiles who would have imagined
small domestic everyday things
like cookers and shower-heads and plant pots
and my geraniums grown from seed flying like
shooting stars
crushing everything made of flesh and burning those
failing to be crushed
missile *missile* yes that's the word and shrapnel that's
another word
in every direction damaging
houses shops and those things we once called *cars*.
Dust cloud in a different life a giant rose rising
higher until the sun is blotted out with flesh and
burning hair everywhere

There followed an eerie silence before the screaming began. Khalid saw part of his son's leg covered in blood. The boy's right shoe was still on his foot, which was a little distance away. The sock was red.

Then the screaming started. It grew louder and shriller. Parents, husbands, wives, shop keepers, all running towards

Khalid their mouths wide open, but he didn't see them. He was busy scooping up his son. He had no idea that he was screaming, too. The boy seemed unconscious, his face burnt on one side, his left arm hanging off at an angle. There was no other complete child in sight; just bits of children.

A man, astride a motorbike, was yelling and gesturing at Khalid.

'Get on the back,' he cried urgently. 'Quickly, let's go! We have to get him to the hospital.'

A string of other motorbikes appeared from nowhere. Khalid stood looking at the man in a crazed way and the man kept on shouting at him to get on the back.

'Now, now! Don't wait for the ambulance. He needs a doctor, *now*.'

Other people were dragging the wounded out of the burning debris as one after another each motorbike sped away in the direction of the town. There was the sound of another explosion somewhere else. Almost instantly ambulances and fire engines could be heard.

Khalid's wife had been in the kitchen preparing the afternoon meal. He wanted to get back to the house, to find her, to see if his other children were alive but the boy in his arms was conscious now and screaming.

Blood dripped from his severed ankle onto Khalid's trousers. The man driving the motorbike was shouting some other instruction but his voice was whipped away.

They passed a roadblock and a roundabout, rendered unrecognisable by the second missile. There was even more chaos here.

Car parts, steering wheels, broken lights, engines on fire and again the huge blocks of concrete where the road had been. Here too there were torsos on fire. The motorcyclist was weaving insanely in and out of the traffic. The child in Khalid's arms was screaming so much that Khalid almost lost his balance as they veered around a corner. He tried to speak to the boy, tried to calm him but only sobs came out of his own mouth.

'Nearly there,' the driver shouted. 'Hold on, one second.'

A moment later they were at the hospital where scores of people were being brought in by car, bike and ambulance. Khalid was off his seat before they came to a standstill. He didn't even thank the driver but staggered up the steps of the building like a drunk. Then he was striding through the entrance, pushing past everyone, the injured, the dying, the police, the nurses, everyone in his path. The child's screams had changed. The boy sounded like an animal. He arched his back and tried to throw himself out of Khalid's arms.

Khalid tightened his grip.

Faces rushed past, mouths opened and closed.

A woman in a black scarf with only half a head stared at him.

Eye sockets emptied of their eyes gaped out of other faces.

A doctor bent over a woman.

A nurse tried to stop him but he pushed her away with his elbows so violently that she reeled against the wall, shocked.

The doctor looked up. He saw the boy's face, took in the soaked stump of a leg and stopped what he was doing. He ordered the nurse to get a trolley, shouted for someone else to help the woman he had been treating and ushered Khalid into another room.

Khalid
sees green walls now
a circular light angled over a bed
a drip held above his head
chrome things
white things
spilled bloody things
pomegranate seeds not *that* thought not *again*
Please

The doctor reached for a swab and slowly, with steady concentration, pushed a needle into the boy's arm and held it there.

One second.

Then another followed.

As the terrible screams faded and broke away, as the boy's eyes closed, it was only Khalid's sobbing that could be heard in the room.

'Go outside,' the doctor said. 'We'll do what we can. His arm, the leg… we'll have to take it off from the knee…'

Khalid sobbed louder.

'Be quiet,' the doctor said, firmly; not unkindly. 'He's alive at least. Later he can have a prosthetic.'

Khalid's shoulders shook with the effort of controlling himself. A nurse took his arm and propelled him to the door and he saw the chaos he had just pushed through. The wounded were everywhere; men women, children.

'Fifty dead,' the nurse said. 'Two missiles. Probably NATO.'

'The bastards,' someone shouted, shaking his fists.

And it was at that moment Khalid remembered what he had momentarily forgotten.

His house.

His wife.

And his two older daughters.

The man with the motorbike, Khalid's neighbour, was waiting for him and the nurse left them so he could be told the news. All of them had died instantly.

'No pain, no suffering,' the neighbour said.

Khalid's house had taken the brunt of the Scud.

'Don't go back,' the man advised. 'The road is blocked. In any case you have to wait for your son to come round from the operation, yes?'

Khalid stared at him and then his phone started to ring. The sound of it was surreal, from a world he had just exited. The sound pulled him backwards to this now defunct reality. Without thinking he searched his pocket and he saw the blood on his clothes. The phone stopped ringing even as he answered it and through the noise and crying and the terrible injuries all around he saw the doctor walking towards him.

> Now it is ending thinks Khalid now I won't forget your face
> Now we are together in this you and I
> Now we are sharing this moment like a glass of sweet tea or a sweetmeat or a butchered lamb
> Now the final horror begins and we are together in this stretched and distorted and sewn up together and I wait for the slap on my face and the push that sends me to the ground and stops me breathing and opens up my mouth
> Screams like cigarette smoke waft
> Everything slows down and I see all the details the blood on his coat
> Read the expression in the doctor's eyes
> The death of hope
> Three times the cock crows out its betrayal
> Doctors are meant to save lives
> The doctor is struggling with gravity.
> In the distance, a long, low, oboe note of other ambulances passing by and the television crew arriving.

They buried Khalid's son at dawn. It was a pink morning, soft as a woman's arms, with swarms of small birds wheeling in the sky. A normal sort of day for some. The call from a distant minaret rose and fell. The doctor found time to witness the funeral.

'He didn't suffer afterwards,' he said.

It was all the comfort he could offer but at least *he* could speak with authority. As the child was only three years old the grave was quite small. Someone, perhaps it was a neighbour, took the boy's foot, still in its shoe, and stuffed it under the shroud. Of Khalid's wife and other children there was no information, although a woman nearby told Khalid she had sold his wife a kilo of pomegranates on the morning of the attack.

At a harbour near Tripoli. 12 September 2015

It was the doctor who paid for Khalid's passage. The doctor could not explain why he did it and Khalid had no idea why he had agreed to go. It was just one of those random acts that happen from time to time. The doctor had told him what was about to take place and Khalid simply did as he was told. He had no interest one way or the other but followed the stream of life towards the point of departure. It took three days before he reached the makeshift harbour. He had only seen the sea once before and for a moment he was aware that it was blue, and beautiful, just like his dead son's eyes. Had he lived the boy would have been fifteen by now. Maybe they would have been on the boat together. Undoubtedly the boy's mother and sisters would have been with them too. Khalid and his wife had often talked about the island that rose up, brown and rugged above the Mediterranean Sea. Now he squashed the thought as though it were a fly.

The sea did not show its treacherous side until they were out of sight of land. All waves behave differently when they are far from the shore. Now these waves rose and fell and the crying started in earnest. They were travelling in a small rubber dinghy that had sprung a sudden leak. Khalid was the only person on board who had no one to hold on to. Alone in this packed boat with the tilting horizon he rode the waves like a surfer. He had nothing left to lose except his thoughts. Suddenly the dinghy capsized and he was taken aback by the fierceness of his terror.

He did not want to die.

> The waves slapped him hard and they muffled the cries of the people
> The waves beat against him again and again with murderous intent
> Death brought his whole life into view with cold wet bitter salty remembrances
> of high days and holidays as in confused horror
> he saw his family their young happy faces coming up from the sea
> Now their voices were rising falling rocking and struggling to be heard
> as the huge wide expanse of sky above his throat
> urged him to remember remember
> remember.
> Water carries memories in its fast flowing currents
> I am going under he thought
> Now it is beginning now I shall give up the struggle
> now I shall give up the broken terrible piece of my world.

He was deceiving himself.

He did not want to die.

The lifeboat came. It rode amongst the bodies floating all around. Amongst the bobbing heads of the dead rocking on the surface of the water, the women clutching the dead children, the men clutching their sons, the small boys with white, wet socks. The boat carefully steered through this.

Orange life jackets amongst the dead.

He was saved.

He was far away from the glittering dome of his mosque.

Then they buried the dead in a small plot by the harbour. No one knew their names but all knew, somewhere in Syria and Libya and elsewhere the mothers would wait for news that would never come.

Those who had saved him vanished and Khalid began the long trek through an indifferent Europe, green now with autumn rain. He watched the countryside pass slowly, watched those younger than himself eager to take on the authorities, the razor sharp fences, the abuse. He walked slowly into time, sleeping when it was dark, rising to start up again at first light. He carried very little into this new life, only those few things that had survived the water.

A wristwatch belonging to his wife. Time was still ticking under its broken glass. No bomb could stop that.

The damp photographs in his wallet randomly taken at some other time.

A small shoe.

Some money his mother had pressed on him. He would never see her again even though they were linked by pain.

A green cloth stained with blood from that past life. How long would the stain last?

Some soap.

His rucksack was light, unlike his life.

Everything Khalid did on the trek was small. He ate little, talked less, smiled not at all. Once a man from England making a television programme fell in step alongside him. When asked, he told the man, what had been broken could not be fixed.

'Why England?' the journalist asked.

Khalid did not know. He had wanted to die, he *still* wanted to die. So why couldn't he? The man, a journalist, walked off a little way and then returned with some bread and tomatoes and in spite of himself Khalid ate hungrily.

Guilt was mixed in with the food but he ate without caring. He was alive and his family were not but still his body made its own imperious demands. His body held him hostage.

The journalist gave him money. The food fed Khalid's guilt and the money the man's. Was guilt a sin, he asked this man who shook his head helplessly.

While they had been walking the landscape had been changing. Vast plains gave way to rolling fields. It was still hot for this time of year and the rough paths they trod meandered through boundaries carved out after another almost-forgotten war. The journalist told Khalid the tracks they walked were ancient; others had fled along these paths.

'My ancestors fled on this route during the war,' he said. 'Carrying their bundles with them, fleeing from different chambers of death.'

Khalid said nothing. For him exodus was part of life.

'I wanted to see for myself what such a journey was like,' the man said.

Hearing these words Khalid looked at the journalist's face. And for the first time a faint glimmer of a smile crossed his own.

It was late afternoon of this fifth day of their trek and the sun was moving westward. The day was nearing its end. High overhead a large bird glided, large and slow and golden as an angel. The sky was still clear but a milk-white fog was forming in the woods. Twisting itself into small pockets the mist thrust out small tongues. Ahead of them was a woman with her head covered in black. Khalid noticed her and was reminded of his dead wife. The woman strayed off the path into the trees and Khalid had a strong impulse to follow her and bring her back but before he could formulate the thought and turn it into action there was a blood-curdling scream. Some of the people in the long straggling line stopped walking, lifted themselves out of their apathy, and went to investigate. They found the woman rotating slowly on the branch of a tree.

'Don't look,' the journalist shouted in warning but it was too late.

Khalid had looked.

Evening was falling and the last train from the border would be leaving soon. The last shreds of the sunset still lingered and they would have to work fast. Someone found a spade in an abandoned cowshed and three of the men dug a hole and buried the woman. In death she continued to remind Khalid of his wife.

'Remember this world is just a corridor,' someone cried in warning.

'But who *are* we Muslims?' asked another.

Khalid had a sudden sharp memory of his wife. She had fallen into his life like ripe fruit falls from a tree. He remembered her with her face thrown back, laughing on that day when their son was born.

'The Muslims are people,' he murmured.

Some time later they arrived at the station and were packed into a train taking them north and Khalid lost sight of the journalist and his cameraman. The carriage was full of distressing sounds and the countryside was shrouded in darkness as once again they waded through time and space. There were no stars for several nights.

Calais. 30 September 2015

It rained for seven days and nights and the mud was everywhere. Khalid shared a tent with twelve men listening to their conversation from a great distance. Time on this occasion stood still. For seven days the twelve men talked. They had twelve different ways of dealing with their situation. Only Khalid had no view. Once he had wished to die but now he was beyond wishes.

'You are in shock,' one of the men observed.

'You need to fight for your country,' another said. 'Kill a few of these Western bastards so they know what it's like for us.'

Khalid thought of the journalist and his cameraman and how they had stood head bowed crying as they buried the Muslim woman.

And he thought of his dead wife. He thought about her for so long and with such force that his thoughts blurred and buckled.

He remembered their courtship.

And the first time he saw her without her veil, on their wedding night and during all the thousands of nights that followed until her untimely death.

He thought of her voice as she sang lullabies to the children when they were tiny and could not sleep.

He thought again of her ready laughter when their son was born.

And when he teased her.

And when she teased him.

'How do I look?' she would ask every time she veiled herself before a trip out.

She would stare at herself in the mirror and say, 'I look like a fat old woman in this!'

'Good!' he'd say. 'Good no one sees your true beauty!'

'You are not fat and you are not old,' their eldest daughter would say.

And then they would laugh; all together. For all that was wrong in their country they had been happy. Then the war was declared and they had listened bewildered to the radio, their hearts heavy with fear. But nothing had prepared them for the terror it would bring. Until powers bigger than themselves had disturbed their fragile equilibrium with their daily bombing, they had thought they would survive.

'Why don't you say something, Khalid?' one of the men in the Camp asked.

Khalid saw that this man was different from the others. He was not a man who had suffered personal tragedy yet his anger was great. He quoted the Koran but he made mistakes, as if he did not know it too well. As if someone had given him a condensed version of that great holy book, but stripped bare and with the beauty taken out. Khalid shook his head. Something of his earlier self flickered like a broken light before switching off again.

A woman from a local charity arrived. She had a box of pomegranates that she offered them. Khalid shook his head but the woman insisted he take one. When he broke it open the juice ran down his hands in dark rivulets. A Government official came to their tent to speak to them.

'You, you, and you,' the official said.

He was not unkind, just matter-of-fact. Khalid was one of those chosen to leave the Camp. And the man who could not quote the Koran correctly was another. The Government official took them away to another tent for questioning. He needed to be sure their thoughts were pure and that they would not cause trouble in this new country. He wanted to be sure they would respect this place that was not their home.

'Of course we will be loyal to our new country,' the man who did not know the Koran said.

He raised his face towards the sky and Khalid saw his eyes glint in the light. Although they looked alike Khalid had a vague sense they were not. Underneath, their brokenness took different forms.

The Government official nodded. It was his unfortunate job to find out how stable the refugees were; how much pain they could withstand without becoming monsters. His job was long and arduous. After he had finished interviewing the men and satisfied himself they were safe to be allowed into the country, the Government official sighed deeply. Then, with a clear conscience, he went off to eat his lunch.

A. L. Kennedy
THE MIGRANTS

When I first wrote this lecture a summary of my argument could have been – when art fails, there is cruelty, because cruelty in humans is caused by a lack of imagination. There are not enough human beings who are ill in the appropriate kinds of ways to individually create epidemic levels of cruelty. They can do harm. Of course. But to do great harm, cruel societies, cultures of cruelty have to be created – either by accident or design, usually both – so that they can recruit otherwise normal human beings to be cruel, even though they might not be under other circumstances. That is to say – when art fails, failure of imagination follows and thereafter cruelty thrives.

Arts practitioners might reply that they are oppressed by the cruel who very reasonably seek to avoid the possible beneficial effects of art escaping into the wider community. This is true.

But it is also true that failure of the arts, of artists, helps the cruel among us triumph and begin to oppress us all, even in relatively free societies, including – and perhaps initially – those who are communicators.

Between my first draft and my last a photograph of a small, dead boy made it to the headlines of many newspapers which had, only hours before, been pouring out hatred at refugees as a moral, cultural, biological and spiritual threat. As David Cameron put it, 'a swarm of people'.

When people are in a swarm, they aren't people. They are both of an alien species and a danger.

When words put them in a swarm, they don't receive the real world's help.

The Paris atrocities haven't happened yet. Because they do happen in Paris, rather than Kenya, DRC, Mexico or South Beirut, they will be exhaustively reported. Outrage will pass seamlessly into cries for escalated violence to meet escalated violence, for the denouncement of all responses which do not involve high explosives. And, of course, the suspicion that this must be the result of the swarm, an evil it has hidden among all its evils, will spring up before it is contradicted by any facts. Belgium will not be carpet-bombed, but Syria must. The convolutions of Russian and Western involvement in the area must not be examined, the interests of the Saudis, or Assad, the possibility of mistakes that could lead to overt, rather than covert war, a conflict of puppeteers, rather than puppets – to discuss such things will be portrayed as weakness. There must be bombing, blood must answer blood.

But for a few days, held between *Je Suis Charlie* and *Nous Sommes Paris*, Europe was looking at the picture of a boy. And we were not the boy, but we somehow allowed ourselves to know him. This is perhaps because he looked like many other little European boys. Boys like beaches and sand and the sea – only this little boy in Western-style dress was dead and face down. He was at once familiar – a boy's body at rest – and horribly changed – a lifeless body, face down, caught in a moment of helpless return to the material. We could easily imagine him as human and alive and not swarming. He developed a name – Aylan Kurdi – and stopped being part of a swarm. The others who died in his boat – including his brother – were brought a little closer to not swarming. His parents developed names and they stopped swarming. These people came to be regarded as people. They were imagined as human. The imagination of the public understood little kids and beaches, cradling little bodies, their limbs heavy with tiredness, not death. That imagination swung towards no longer regarding the human beings camped at Calais in miserable conditions and occasionally being crushed or drowned or smothered trying to reach the UK as people who might have been kids and played, kids who weren't necessarily born to be an existential threat.

Our media may or may not have been permitted this change of tone because of public disgust at increasingly repellent coverage, online petitions and the like. Or else because the UK and other Western European governments – having been unable to wish away the humanitarian crisis they helped create and to hide its human impact behind a screen of more or less racist abuse – had decided to change tack. So many countries with so many arms to sell, so many politicians with so much to distract us from, such a need to seem competent and decisive – bringing additional war to Syria was something they found inviting. Public pressure had prevented an earlier move to bring on more war in an already war-torn area. The possibility that our Western, noble war would stop people fleeing the unpleasant, foreign type of war in Syria was being promoted. If a number of arms manufacturers would make a great deal of money in the process, that would be coincidental. After Paris, the logic would be that all refugees were potential terrorists and that blowing up neighbourhoods and civilians would in no way act to aid the grooming and recruitment of more young men and women with ruined futures and an awareness of current events. But – in the space between *Je Suis* and *Nous Sommes* – maybe a little dead kid could make us want to blow up other little kids whose names we would never know and who we would never see, lying down and little and dead. If our imaginations were focused on strident and powerful (if quite vague) solutions and not on children scattered in pieces, or on fire and if we could imagine that other, still alive kids might one day play on their own beaches in their homelands – or else in happy sand (don't Muslim kids enjoy sand, anyway, haven't we heard that somewhere...?), then money could be made. We could imagine people (perhaps kids) thanking us for blowing up some of the people who were blowing them up in such a way that everything turned out well in the end. We were not encouraged to remember imaginings of this kind in the run-up to the invasion and occupation of Iraq. We were not encouraged to remember the invasion and occupation of Iraq.

So, at the time of Aylan, the swarm was no longer quite the swarm it was. The ambient hatred of the Other changed focus slightly. The media around us (which are increasingly distrusted and ignored and therefore increasingly strident and toxic) spent time worrying a little about VW exhaust emissions, rather more about David Beckham's marriage and very much more about the strangely beige and gentle threat of Jeremy Corbyn – a candidate the media didn't back and whose existence they find perplexing. The massive displacement of human beings from their homes all across Europe and the Middle East was rarely examined in anything like depth, or presented as being perhaps of more importance than a variety of celebrity talent competitions and soap operas. The humanity of refugees, emigrants, or for that matter David Beckham and Jeremy Corbyn, the humanity of our responses is allowed or encouraged to fade. As usual.

Imagination is, on all sides, apparently failing. And when it fails, it fails us all. What do we artists do now? Because we must be responsive, surely – we must somehow be guardians of imagination, of wider thought, of culture. What have we done wrong? What did we forget? What can we do now?

True art is not an indulgence, but a fundamental defence of humanity. We seem condemned to forget, to learn and to forget this truth. Each time we do, some of us die. Those defined as Others go first. The strangers, the migrants, those forced into desperate motion by cascading cruelties: we ignore them to death, torment them to confirm our own prejudices. Dominant regimes around the world may simply execute whole families by remote control. Nonetheless, all those people – the harmed, the running and the dead – they are us. Harming others recoils upon us. Morally, creatively, environmentally, literally, ignoring this fact means that we have entered into a murder-suicide pact with ourselves.

Let us consider the idea of the artist as a kind of eternal, voluntary migrant from the far-off territories of the engaged mind, the superior imagination. What use is that in these dark times? How do we save lives? How do we render lives secure? Is that even what an artist wishes to do?

I would argue that any artist practising their art at a high level of technical skill and realisation will be defending human beings. The effect of art is inherently beneficial, unless it is actively shaped to a malign agenda – and that agenda will usually damage the effectiveness of the art. Because fully functional art is about the irreplaceability of the human experience and its communality, it helps save us all. But we probably no longer live in a time when simply practising our art is enough. All over the world – and even countries which see themselves as harbouring free expression and democracy – artistic expression is on the retreat and inhumanity at every level is apparently increasing. This is, in part, a falsehood produced by a media industry addicted to shock and illusion, but certainly worldwide conflict, pandemic disease, imposed poverty and debt are all producing their predictable results – despair, rage, death, violence, intellectual struggle and bewilderment, nihilism.

Speaking as a writer, I am used – perhaps too used – to our role as someone occupying a moral high ground, supposedly seeing clearly and then speaking wisely on behalf of our societies, our species. Powerful and thoughtful writing are, of course, hugely beneficial. They give rise to new imaginings, better futures, the framing of laws. They sustain us in our solitude. And new technologies are joining together the well-disposed peoples of the world as never before. We can discover each other's pains faster than ever. We can supersede old and corrupted journalistic models. We can write to the fullest extent of our abilities in order to show ourselves the depth of our beauty, the irreplaceable gift of each life. But this may not be enough any more.

I feel we need to rediscover and restate our full potential as artists, our roles in shaping and creating cultures and the debt we owe to those cultures which still harbour us, which allow us our louder-than-average voices. If we know what we truly are, we can fully be what we are.

Mass culture in Europe and around the world is increasingly addicted to wealth and loathing and its incessant prioritisation and promotion. Shoddy, debased and debasing propaganda overwhelms by dint of its sheer, grinding, global repetition. And yet, for generations we have been able to identify the precursors of catastrophic violence in human societies, of violence against groups and individuals. We know that strict control and suppression of humanising art, the control of manifest joys, the rationing of shared pleasures – these all mark the beginning of a process which ends in hell.

The minimisation and silencing of art from individuals and groups classified as Other combines with and complements mass media attacks on those groups. Real life migrants – rather than we voluntary outcasts – are easy targets. In the UK, those who have been evicted from their homelands by the consequences of our economic and military policies are now blamed for their homelessness. To paraphrase Colin Powell – we broke it but we don't want to fix it. Within many societies, the only response to pain and grief is a condemnation of its victims. In the UK, our summer headlines framed a crisis which saw utterly desperate human beings even trying to swim the English Channel as a torment for delayed British holiday makers. Radio phone-ins played up the threat of illegal immigrants numbering in their hundreds as a horde that would overwhelm our whole culture. The same culture that has spent decades expelling art from its discourse and from its financial blessing has embraced loathing. Theresa May, Britain's controversial Home Secretary, alarmed the Institute of Directors and surprised the UK's Migration Advisory Committee by using her address to the 2015 Conservative Party Conference to deny the positive effects of immigration and repeat a number of allegations about job-stealing, healthcare clogging immigrants which simply aren't true. Hoping to shape our imaginations into a state of fear from which she could then save us.

But history teaches us that our greatest wrongs, crimes against humanity and genocide, arise from cultures where hatred has become a part of the air citizens breathe. When imagination fails, a culture fails, a society fails, a nation fails and then – perhaps – later there will be lawyers, some attempt to establish truth, guilt, reconciliation. Establishing what is termed 'intent to destroy' when we try to prosecute individuals for crimes against humanity and genocide is often hugely difficult precisely because of the political pronouncements, media activity and propaganda that shape and then dominate sick cultures. In a hate-filled culture, a nation's sense of self becomes grounded on those it despises. True citizenship becomes a narrower and narrower concept – and without its safety death stalks ever closer.

Clearly, all interested parties including writers and artists must act in the UK and elsewhere. And we are attempting to organise, to rediscover the faith in ourselves as a species and as workers for the survival of that species. But we are pressured by a raft of new negative forces. We know that around the world press freedoms are being smothered. Attacks may be verbal, legal, physical, financial, subtle or overt. The effect is always chilling, silencing. Even in relatively 'free' nations slashed rates of pay, collapsed print media, demands for free content and the toxic effects of the so-called War on Terror mean that writers are censored, or self-censor. Some are simply silenced by exhaustion. But I will say again that without artists, and perhaps writers in particular, human beings are easier to destroy, first in effigy, then in part, then as a totality. Groups and individuals trust their immortality to their cultural creations – removing access to their dignity and presence in the world makes it easier to destroy them. We Honorary Others must respond now as never before – not least because a threat to one group really is eventually a threat to all.

Real-world migrants are now among a growing number of stridently defined Others. At a global level we're seeing a decline or removal of rights for women, workers, the disabled, those with a mental illness, the poor and the imprisoned. Information from expensive sources like investigative journalism has collapsed. Gossip and controversy corrupt the public discourse while internet communities form coral reefs of solipsistic myth and confirmation. Sharpening redefinitions of loyalty and identity are bringing about a conflict between sovereign states and corporate states. Old-style nationalisms of loathing and exclusion are condemned by corporate media that borrow and promote their agendas. Meanwhile, nationalism as an expression of non-corporate identity, cultural choice and personal diversity may offer a reclamation of citizens' rights and a resurgence of cultural expression.

There are many examples of united cultures full of difference that succeed, of communities accepting and defending their new members. A global cultural landscape, within which the inaccuracies of *Zero Dark Thirty* can justify torture, or we can watch online executions in jumpsuits of competing colours, or see the *Merkelstreichelt* (Merkel stroke) offer hopeless sympathy, needs all the positive examples it can get.

To reference the UK, while – for example – working-class communities in Glasgow fight to keep adopted immigrant families from arbitrary deportation, our media rant about 'hard-workers' and 'spongers', about endless alien threats. A government beset by hideous sex scandals and doggedly pursuing a social and economic agenda best suited to an invading power has sought to distract us from the pains they cause us, by blaming them on Others. Our new Independent Press Standards Organisation can currently induce apologies (in small print) when errors of fact have occurred. Most attacks are framed in fact-free outbursts of rage.

Over the last two decades in the UK mainstream media articles have repeatedly linked migrants to disease and all manner of crime. Zeid Ra'ad Al Hussein, UN Commissioner for Human Rights, recently characterised Europe as having 'a nasty underbelly of racism' which skews our response to genuine human need. He made particular reference to the UK and our self-styled commentator, Katie Hopkins. Like a number of similar figures, Hopkins seeks to generate outrage in order to get attention, website 'clicks'. She has a background in PR and the military and rose to fame on a TV reality show. This is an almost perfect path to prominence in many unwary and fading democracies. Research, facts, quality writing – they require funding, effort, ability. Confirming of readers' prejudices is easier. UK surveys repeatedly show that responders massively overestimate numbers of fraudulent benefit claims and immigrant Others – this error is substantially a mass media creation. It is a nightmare of alien rapaciousness, created by the media's mass imagination. Mr Al Hussein highlighted Hopkins's description of migrants 'spreading like norovirus on a cruise ship'. She called them 'cockroaches' – echoing Rwanda's Radio Mille Collines and its exhortations to genocide.

Commercialised hate on a global scale means it's no surprise that trafficking people for gain, using them as slaves, as product, is – like warfare – a growing business. What figures we can gather from sources like the UN and the US State Department suggest that people trafficking blights millions of lives and generates income in the tens, if not hundreds, of billions of dollars every year. (Slaves, like oil, are valued in dollars.) The industry affects more than 20 million people. Not cockroaches. People. And, beyond punishing migrants, the UK government removes support from those with special needs and mental health difficulties, the homeless, poor, old, young, sick… Each of us is sullied by some aspect of this cruelty. An institutionally racist police force, an underfunded legal system and a prison industry geared to increase reoffending and profits hide some of the consequences while increasing others. As in so many fading democracies, manifestations of mercy rely on groups and individuals having internalised values other than those in the ascendant.

But in a world of Avaaz, aid volunteers and charity crowdfunding, a world where 15 million marched against a war in Iraq on behalf of strangers who couldn't, there are alterative models for humanity. As writers and artists we have experienced the fact that art is stronger than propaganda, that love is stronger and more sustainable than hate, that self-expression can mean more than self-indulgence. We have values. This dark time can teach us about light. We have the capacity to offer a vast variety and depth of human information. We can make dreams to lead mankind forward and expressions of individuality that can make many free. Without those dreams, we face only nightmares. We must do better.

Let us, together, imagine the future – if we don't, it will happen without us and may kill us along the way.

This is an updated version of the opening lecture of the European Literature Days festival given by A. L. Kennedy in Spitz, Austria, on 23 October 2015.

BIOGRAPHIES

Hassan Abdulrazzak is of Iraqi origin, born in Prague and living in London. Hassan's first play, *Baghdad Wedding*, was staged at Soho Theatre in 2007 to great acclaim. *The Prophet* was performed at the Gate Theatre in 2012. He has been published in the *Guardian*, *Edinburgh Review*, *Banipal*, *Niqash*, *Arab Stages* and *Snakeskin*. Hassan's latest play, *Love, Bombs and Apples*, was staged at the Arcola Theatre in June 2015 as part of the Shubbak festival and will enjoy a second run in 2016.

Nick Barlay is the author of four novels, including *Hooky Gear*, which was included in Granta's list of Best Young British Novelists in 2003. His first non-fiction book is *Scattered Ghosts*, the story of his Hungarian Jewish family over two centuries. It was longlisted for the Wingate Prize 2015. He has also written short stories, award-winning radio plays and wide-ranging journalism. He regularly teaches creative writing, as well as *Guardian* Masterclasses in writing family history.

Sebastian Barry was born in Dublin in 1955. His novels and plays have won, among other awards, the Kerry Group Irish Fiction Prize, the Costa Book of the Year Award, the Irish Book Awards Best Novel, the Independent Booksellers Prize and the James Tait Black Memorial Prize. He also had two consecutive novels, *A Long Long Way* and *The Secret Scripture*, shortlisted for the Man Booker Prize, in 2005 and 2008 respectively.

William Boyd is the author of fourteen novels, including *A Good Man in Africa*, winner of the Whitbread Literary Award and the Somerset Maugham Award; *An Ice Cream War*, winner of the John Llewellyn Rhys Prize and shortlisted for the Booker Prize; *Any Human Heart*, winner of the Prix Jean Monnet; and *Restless*, winner of the Costa Novel of the Year Award, the *Yorkshire Post* Novel of the Year Award and a Richard & Judy selection. His latest, *Sweet Caress*, was published in 2015.

Kate Clanchy was born and grew up in Scotland and now lives in Oxford. Her poetry collections *Slattern, Samarkand* and *Newborn* have brought her many literary awards and been widely acclaimed. She is also the author of *Antigona and Me, Meeting the English* and a short story collection, *The Not-Dead and the Saved*, published in 2015. She has written extensively for Radio 4.

Amanda Craig was born in South Africa in 1959, and brought up in Italy and Britain. After reading English at Clare College, Cambridge, she became the author of six interlinked novels, which deal with contemporary British society, the most recent of which is *Hearts and Minds*. Amanda has just completed her seventh novel, set in Devon and London.

Moris Farhi was born in Ankara, Turkey, in 1935 and came to the UK in 1954. His novels include: *The Pleasure of Your Death* (1972); *The Last of Days* (1983); *Journey through the Wilderness* (1989); *Children of the Rainbow* (1999); *Young Turk* (2004); and *A Designated Man* (2009). His collection of poems, *Songs from Two Continents*, was published in 2011. He is a Fellow of both the Royal Society of Literature and the Royal Geographical Society and a Vice President of International PEN. In 2001, he was appointed an MBE for 'services to literature'.

Elaine Feinstein is a prize-winning poet, novelist, playwright, biographer and translator. Her first novel, *The Circle* (1970), was longlisted for the 'lost' Man Booker Prize in 2010. Alive to her family origins in the Russian-Jewish diaspora, she developed a close affinity with the Russian poets of this and the last century. Her versions of the poems of Marina Tsvetaeva were a *New York Times* Book of the Year. Her biography of Anna Akhmatova, *Anna of all the Russias,* has been translated into twelve languages. *It Goes with the Territory: Memoirs of a Poet* was published in 2013 and her most recent book of poems is *Portraits* (Carcanet, 2015).

Tim Finch's debut novel, *The House of Journalists,* was published by Jonathan Cape in 2013. A writer and consultant, Tim is currently acting as the co-ordinator of the new National Refugee Welcome Board. He was previously director of communications at the Institute for Public Policy Research and at the Refugee Council, and before that was a BBC journalist for many years.

Sue Gee's novels include *The Hours of the Night, The Mysteries of Glass,* longlisted for the 2005 Orange Prize for Fiction, *Reading in Bed* and *Coming Home.* She is also the author of many short stories. Sue is a mentor with the Write to Life group at Freedom from Torture, and teaches at the Faber Academy. Her new novel, *Trio,* is published by Salt.

Stephen Kelman was born in Luton in 1976. His first novel, *Pigeon English,* was shortlisted for the Man Booker Prize in 2011, as well as the *Guardian* First Book Award, the Desmond Elliott Prize and a Galaxy National Book Award. It is a featured title on the AQA GCSE English Literature syllabus. His second novel, *Man on Fire,* was published in 2015.

A. L. Kennedy was born in Dundee in 1965. She is the author of seventeen books: six literary novels, one science fiction novel, seven short story collections and three works of non-fiction. She was twice included in the Granta Best of Young British Novelists list. She has won awards including the 2007 Costa Book Award and the Austrian State Prize for International Literature. She is also a dramatist for the stage, radio, TV and film. She is an essayist and regularly reads her work on BBC Radio. She occasionally writes and performs one-person shows.

Hanif Kureishi's novels include *The Buddha of Suburbia, The Black Album, Intimacy* and *The Last Word*. His short story collections include *Love in a Blue Time, Midnight All Day* and *The Body*. His screenplays include *My Beautiful Laundrette, Sammy and Rosie Get Laid, My Son the Fanatic* and *Le Week-End*. Among his other publications are the collection of essays *Dreaming and Scheming, The Word and the Bomb, Love + Hate,* the memoir *My Ear at His Heart* and the essay *A Theft: My Con Man.*

Marina Lewycka was born in a refugee camp in Germany in 1946 and moved to England with her family when she was about a year old. Her debut novel *A Short History of Tractors in Ukrainian* was shortlisted for the Orange Prize and went on to sell over a million copies in thirty-five languages. This was followed by *Two Caravans, We Are All Made of Glue* and *Various Pets Alive and Dead*. She is a trustee of Counterpoint Arts, a charity dedicated to promoting creative arts by and about refugees and migrants in the UK.

Hubert Moore is a poet with eight published poetry collections, including *The Hearing Room* and *Beautifully Kept Things*. Hubert spent nine years as a writing mentor with the Write to Life group at the Medical Foundation for the Care of Victims of Torture, now Freedom from Torture. His most recent collections are *Whistling Back* and *The Bright Gaze of the Disoriented*, both published by Shoestring.

Courttia Newland is the author of seven works of fiction including his debut, *The Scholar*. His latest, *The Gospel According to Cane*, was published in 2013 and has been optioned by Cowboy Films as a TV serial. He was nominated for the Impac Dublin Literary Award and the Frank O'Connor International Short Story Award, among others. His short stories have appeared in many anthologies and been broadcast on Radio 4. As a playwright he has been nominated for the Alfred Fagon Award and the Theatre503 Playwriting Award. He is an associate lecturer in creative writing at Birkbeck, University of London and is completing a PhD in creative writing.

Ruth Padel is a poet and novelist, and teaches poetry at King's College London. She has published nine poetry collections, a novel and eight books of non-fiction, including three on reading poetry. Her most recent collection, *Learning to Make an Oud in Nazareth*, is on the Middle East, with poems on all three Abrahamic religions; *The Mara Crossing* is a mixed-genre meditation on migration in prose and poetry. Her awards include First Prize in the UK National Poetry Competition, a Cholmondeley Award from the Society of Authors, an Arts Council of England Writers' Award and a British Council Darwin Now Research Award for her novel *Where the Serpent Lives*.

Katharine Quarmby is a writer, journalist and film-maker specialising in social affairs, education, foreign affairs and politics, with an investigative and campaigning edge.

Her first book for adults, *Scapegoat: Why We Are Failing Disabled People* (Portobello Press), won the Ability Media Literature Award in 2011. In 2012, Katharine was shortlisted for the Paul Foot Award for campaigning journalism, by the *Guardian* and *Private Eye*, for her five years of campaigning against disability hate. Her latest book is *No Place to Call Home: Inside the Real Lives of Gypsies and Travellers* (Oneworld Publications).

Noo Saro-Wiwa was born in Nigeria and raised in England. Her debut book, *Looking for Transwonderland: Travels in Nigeria* (Granta, 2012), was selected as BBC Radio 4's Book of the Week, named *The Sunday Times* Travel Book of the Year in 2012, shortlisted for the Authors' Club Dolman Travel Book of the Year Award and was nominated by the *Financial Times* as one of the best travel books of 2012. The *Guardian* included it among its 10 Best Contemporary African Books in 2012. It has been translated into French and Italian. Noo has written for the *Guardian*, the *Independent*, the *Financial Times*, the *Times Literary Supplement* and *Prospect* magazine. She lives in the UK.

Joan Smith is a novelist, columnist and campaigner for human rights. She has been co-chair of the Mayor of London's Violence Against Women and Girls Panel since 2013, and is a former chair of the English PEN Writers in Prison Committee. She has published six novels, including the Loretta Lawson series of crime novels, and the feminist classic *Misogynies*. Her latest book is *Down with the Royals* (Biteback).

Roma Tearne is a Sri Lankan-born novelist and film-maker living in the UK. She left Sri Lanka with her family at the start of the civil unrest during the 1960s. She has written six novels. Her fifth, *The Road to Urbino*, was published by

Little, Brown in June 2012 to coincide with the premiere of her film of that name at the National Gallery in London. She has been shortlisted for the Costa First Novel Award, the Kirimaya and *LA Times* Book Prize and longlisted for the Orange Prize in 2011 and the Asian Man Booker Prize in 2012. Her sixth novel, *The Last Pier,* was published in April 2015.

Rose Tremain's novels and short stories have been published worldwide and won many prizes, including the *Sunday Express* Book of the Year Award (for *Restoration,* also shortlisted for the Booker Prize); the Prix Femina Etranger (for *Sacred Country*); the Whitbread Novel of the Year Award (for *Music & Silence*); and the Orange Prize for Fiction 2008 (for *The Road Home*). *Restoration* was filmed in 1995 and a stage version was produced in 2009. More recently, *Merivel: A Man of His Time* was shortlisted for both the Walter Scott Prize and the Wellcome Trust Prize. Her latest collection of short stories, *The American Lover,* was published in November 2014 and her new novel, *The Gustav Sonata,* was published in May 2016.

Alex Wheatle was born to Jamaican parents living in Brixton in 1963. He spent most of his childhood in a Surrey children's home. His first novel, *Brixton Rock,* was published to critical acclaim in 1999. Five more novels, *East of Acre Lane, The Seven Sisters, Island Songs, Brenton Brown* and *The Dirty South,* followed, all highly praised, and his books are on school reading lists. His latest novel, *Liccle Bit,* was published in 2015 and was nominated for a Carnegie Medal.

ACKNOWLEDGEMENTS

My heartfelt thanks to all the wonderful contributors who have made this anthology. Thanks also to those who helped in the early stages – Cat Lucas from English PEN, Tom Green and Almir Koldzic from Counterpoint Arts, Freedom from Torture, the Refugee Council, Free Word, and my agent Andrew Lownie. Thanks also to Mitch Albert, Faz Fazali, Andrew Newton, Cheryl Pierce, Caroline Williams, and Meike Ziervogel. Thanks to Olga Stachowska who produced my pitch video for the Unbound website, and finally thank you to all at Unbound, particularly DeAndra Lupu, Philip Connor, Georgia Odd, Jason Cooper, Caitlin Harvey, and Amy Winchester.

Abacus, 2012, © Roma Tearne. Reproduced by permission of the author. Her story 'The Colour of Pomegranates' is from her unpublished novel *Whitewash*, © Roma Tearne.

Rose Tremain's contribution is an extract from her short story 'The Beauty of the Dawn Shift', which appears in the collection *The Darkness of Wallis Simpson*, published by Vintage Books, Random House, 2005, © Rose Tremain. Reproduced by permission of Sheil Land Associates Ltd.

SUPPORTERS

Unbound is a new kind of publishing house. Our books are funded directly by readers. This was a very popular idea during the late eighteenth and early nineteenth centuries. Now we have revived it for the internet age. It allows authors to write the books they really want to write and readers to support the writing they would most like to see published.

The names listed below are of readers who have pledged their support and made this book happen. If you'd like to join them, visit: www.unbound.co.uk.

Harriet and Jason Abbott
Timothy Ades
Tony Aitman
Mitch Albert
Aisling Allardice
Judith Allnatt
Su Allport
Linda Almond
Peter Amlot
Catherine Annabel
Rebecca Armstrong
Michael Atkinson
Ethel Austin
Chris Badman
Sharon Bakar
Jason Ballinger
Alison Bambridge
Maria Banica
Margaret Barnard
Sarah Barnes
Lydia Baron-Lux
Jenny Barrett
Jeannette Baxter
Sonia Beck
Helen Bellany
Lucy Beresford
Paul Berry
Geraldine Blake
Anna Blasiak
Rex Bloomstein
Margaret Bluman
Roger Blunden
Anne Bohbot
Nickie Bonn
Bill Bonwitt
Zamir Borg-Mirza
Marco Borselli
Richard Boulter
Tom Boydell
Tracy Brabin
Andy Brereton
Judi Brill
Tim Bromfield
James Brookes
Carolyn Brown
Laura Brown
Alexandra Büchler
Rosie Buckman
Rebecca Burton
Ceri Butler
Roger Bygott
Jennifer Cairns
Alan Calder
Heather Cameron
Alistair Canlin
Teresa Cannon
Miranda Cansell
Viv Carbines
Chloe Carter
Andrew Catlin
Chris Chalmers
Esme Chandler
Robert Chandler
Priya Changela
Alix Christie
Leslie Clark
Tim Clark
David Clarke & Lucy McCall
Evelyn Clegg
Chantal Rosas Cobian

Steve Collett
Richard Collins
Kieron Connolly
Geraldine Cook
Lucy Corr
Sarah Courtauld
Robyn Cowan
Helen Coyle
John Crawford
Margaret Crick
Louise Cross
Hannah Cullen
Susan Curtis-Kojakovic
Geraldine D'Amico
Adam Dacey
Katrine Dalsgård
Carola Darwin
Emma Darwin
Sophia Darwin
Matt & Owen Davies
Sara Davies
Natalie Del-Mar
Neil Denham
Ferdinand Dennis
Madalena Derwojedowa
Hope Dinsey
Tom Dixon
Roger Dobson
Wendalynn Donnan
Joanna Elding
Liz Evers
Karin Eyben
Moris Farhi
Benedict Farr
Diana Farr
Charlotte Featherstone
Rachel Fidler
Olivia Maya Field
Rose Filippi
Gaddo Flego
James Flint
John-Paul Flintoff
Jaime Foot
Cecilia Foxall
HW Freedman
Alison Freegard
Vivien Gardner
Mandy Garner
Amro Gebreel
Richard George
Ryan Gibberd
Claire Gibbon
Jo Gibson
Jennie Gillions
Carol Godsmark
Rosalind Green
Tom Green
Lenore Greensides
Bedene Greenspan
Sally Griffin
John Griffiths
Caroline Haastrup-Baptiste
Kate Hammer
Barry Hankey
Kim Harries
Caitlin Harvey
James Harvey
Hasani Hasani
Carolyn Hayman
Sheila Hayman
Imogen Heath
Vicky Hempstead
Caroline Henderson
Elaine Henderson
Maria Hennessy
Hermione
Jeanette Hewitt
Davida Highley
Katy Hilditch
Clive Holland
Clare Hopton
Rachel Hore
Ann Horne
Suzy Humphries
Victoria Carew Hunt
Ray Hunter
Jennifer Hurstfield
Majeed Jabbar
Emma Jackson
Jade Jackson
Kerensa Jennings
Emily Jeremiah
Chris Johnson
Jane Johnson
Adam Jones
Heather Jones
Toby Jones
Jill Kaige
Stella Kane
Hilary Kemp
Shama Khan
Fozia Khanam
Patrick Kincaid
James Kingston
Mark Kirkbride
Carina Krause
Jennifer Lamy
Alison Layland
Helen le May
Fiona Ledger
Tracey Lee & Luke Warren
Charlie Lee-Potter
Fiona Linday
Jerry Lockspeiser
Linda Lucas
Brian Lunn
Michelle Macdonald
Philippa Manasseh
Tom Mansfield
Doro Marden
Ed McKeon

Susana Medina
Philip Middleton
Cristina Mindroiu
Clara Ministral
Jitka Minxova
Ronald Mitchinson
Alice Morgan
Edward Mortimer
Ronjon Nag
Helen Nash
Andrew Newton
David Nicholls
Elizabeth Nicholson
Sue Nieland
Maria Nunn
Kevin O'Connor
Jack O'Donnell
Kieron O'Kelly
Brian Oharegreen
Par Olsson
Asta Ottey
Nigel Packer
Sarah Chalmers Page
Tanya Pardoe
Emily Parsons
Kirk Parsons
Lucy Pegler
Becky Penney
Clare Pennington
Jo Pettitt
Robert Phillips
Cheryl Pierce
Edwina Popescu
Philip Popescu
Jenny Priestman
Katharine Quarmby
Stephanie Ressort
Carolyn Reynolds
Paula Richards
Sioned-Mair Richards
Gillian Richmond
Andrea Rippon
Mike Robbins
Mari Roberts
Suzanne Robey
Shaun Rock
Judith Rodriguez
Phil Rose
Alice Sachrajda
Natalie Samarasinghe
Chantal Savignon
Peter Schwartz
Ros Schwartz
Suzanne Scott
Anna Scrine
Luna &
Barley Sefton-Moss
Nicola Shilcock
Emma Simmons
Emi Slater
Kim Slater
Hazel Slavin
Susan Smillie
Helen Smith
Joyce Smith
Kate Smith
Nigel Smith
Patrick Milling Smith
Susan Sandford Smith
Josh Spero
Laura Statham
Henriette B. Stavis
Margaret Stevens
John Stewart-Murray
Amanda Stone
Kay Stuart
Arch Tait
Taro Takahashi
Philomena Tarkowski
Helen Taylor
Joanna Taylor
Lucy Taylor
Margaret Tongue
Abbi Torrance
Lindsay Trevarthen
Tina Tse
Robin Tuddenham
Giles L. Turnbull
Imogen Tyler
Louise Underwood
Marianne Velmans
Mark Vent
Dirk vom Lehn
Jo W
Steve Wake
Brendan Walsh
Lucy Ward
Adam Warn
Nancy Wells
Anna Wesener
David Wheeler
Katie Whitehouse
Mary Wickenden
Annabelle Wilkins
Caroline Williams
Richard Williams
Simon Williams
WomenCentre
Carol Wood
Elli Woollard
Lisa Wren
Meike Ziervogel